THE RIGHT PLACE

A WRITE PLACE RETREAT ROMANCE

MJ COMPTON

COMPTONPLATIONS PUBLISHING

Editor: Jena O'Connor, Practical Proofing

Cover Art: 100 Covers

Published in the United States of America by

Comptonplations Publishing

EBOOK ISBN: 978-1-959923-11-4

PRINT ISBN: 978-1-959923-12-1

www.comptonplations.com

This book is a work of fiction. While reference might be made to actual historical events or existing locations, the names, characters, places, and incidents are either the product of the author's imagination or are used fictitiously, and any resemblance to actual persons, living or dead, business establishments, events, or locales is entirely coincidental.

The publisher does not have any control over and does not assume any responsibility for author or third-party websites or their content.

Contents

CHAPTER ONE

SUNDAY, JUNE 11, 2000

D arby Remington clutched a spiral notebook to her breasts, as she stood on Camp Nippletop's wide porch. The towering pine and cedar trees surrounding the main lodge scented the late spring air. Insects chirped, birds peeped, a breeze rustled the overhead branches. Even after a month, she still couldn't believe she owned a piece of the largest park in the lower 48 states. That she, thanks to a cosmic joke, had inherited an Adirondack Mountain Great Camp.

Darby had always called the High Peaks Region home. Remington roots ran deep in northern New York... not that her relatives included the famous artist from Ogdensburg or the firearms manufacturers in southern Herkimer County. Maybe transforming the Great Camp would be her chance to become an Adirondack legend.

Her property hid in the forest, lurking on the edge of the lake bearing the same name as nearby Nippletop Mountain. She couldn't rename the geography, but her Great Camp needed a new designation.

Her camp. This main lodge, the outbuildings, and guest cabins. If she met all the stipulations outlined in James Coolidge Astin's will, the camp plus significant acreage, including the lake, would be hers.

She wasn't sure she was up to the challenge. Hence the notebook full of lists of what needed to be done before she could fulfill Astin's conditions. She'd already wasted a month debating whether she should accept the inheritance.

The crunch of tires on the dirt drive had her bracing her spine. A female alone in the woods needed to be cautious. While bears and moose were worrisome, humans tended to be more dangerous.

A dark green pickup truck with a wide yellow stripe and "State Forest Ranger" emblazoned on the side pulled up to the porch.

Darby only marginally relaxed. A woman couldn't be too careful. She wished she'd gotten around to buying pepper spray.

He's a cop, she reminded herself as a tall ranger unfolded himself from the truck. *One of the good guys.*

"Good afternoon, ma'am," he said.

Darby didn't trust a man whose eyes she couldn't see, and mirrored sunglasses hid his. "Good afternoon. Is there a problem?"

She didn't know how to address him. The silver bar pinned above his right chest pocket named him Winehouse. Sounded like a fancy tourist destination in Lake George.

"Checking on the property. I heard the camp changed hands recently."

"I'm the new owner." Darby bristled. Although she'd been reluctant to accept the inheritance, once she decided, she'd committed to making Astin's dream come true. "Contact Mr. Astin's attorney. Howard Chatham in Lake Placid. Astin left everything to me."

She hated talking to blank walls. Because she couldn't see his eyes through the reflective lenses of his sunglasses, Ranger Winehouse could have been one of the granite cliffs on the other side of the lake.

"Oh, I believe you." He grinned.

He had nice teeth. A tiny chip in his upper right front tooth added personality.

"Could you take off your shades?" she asked. "Or is wearing them an intimidation technique you learned in ranger school?"

He pulled off the dark-rimmed glasses and hooked them into the vee neck of his shirt. "Better?"

No.

Because without the shades, he morphed from official to attractive.

"Sure." As he strode the distance between his vehicle and the porch, she could tell he didn't have ordinary eyes. They appeared rusty brown, like the iron-rich water in the area's lakes. However, beneath the surface —

"I'm warning everyone in the area about an escapee from the Adirondack Correctional Facility."

Darby stiffened. Only 30 miles separated Ray Brook, site of the medium security prison, from her property. Thirty treacherous miles, but still too close for comfort. Then again, the prison was closer to her apartment in the village of Saranac Lake, where the cluster of civilization forged a false sense of safety.

"Thank you," she said.

"Are you out here alone?" Ranger Winehouse's deep voice tingled along her nerve endings.

Now that was a loaded question.

"Can I see some ID?"

His devastating grin flashed again. "Yes, ma'am." He stopped at the bottom step of the porch and pulled out a leather case. The sun snuck through the overhead branches and glinted off the silvery metal of his shield. The wallet also contained his photo. His name. *Cameron Winehouse.*

"And you are?" His tone remained professionally polite.

She swallowed her reluctance. "Darby Remington."

"Are you out here alone?" Ranger Winehouse repeated his question. "Because if you are, you should also be aware—"

"Bear safety? I grew up around here."

"Yes, ma'am, but I'm talking about the two-legged dangers. Meth labs, marijuana farms, paramilitary cults, and undocumented immigrants smuggled in from Canada. We're monitoring an uptick in suspicious activity lately."

Her brain blanked for a moment. "Meth labs? Undocumented immigrants? Here?"

"You have the ideal set-up—an isolated camp, abandoned outbuildings—"

"I beg your pardon," she interrupted. His assumptions annoyed her. "The outbuildings are not abandoned. They're underutilized. I'm renovating the camp into a writing retreat, per the late James Coolidge Astin's instructions. Nothing illegal is going on."

"I understand, ma'am. Ms. Remington. However, Mr. Astin may not have been aware of the suspicious activity on his property. We're hearing increased chatter."

Ranger Winehouse's suspicions explained the uneasiness she'd experienced while exploring the property. She'd been taught to trust her instincts. Her gut told her something was not right. Ranger Winehouse's warning confirmed her fears.

Cam Winehouse called on all his training to remain professional while confronting the most attractive woman he'd ever seen.

Prickly, too. She needed to be handled with care.

Darby Remington's generous curves defined every place a woman was supposed to be round. Her breasts were like pillows to cushion a man as he fell into her softness at the end of a hard day. When a man grabbed her ass, he'd know he clutched a female.

"I didn't realize forest rangers dealt with drugs." Her doe-like eyes widened. "I thought you tagged deer ticks and stuff."

A sense of humor, too. "Alerting the state police when we find drugs falls into the *and stuff* category."

She smiled, and it was as if the sun had fallen to earth in order to illuminate the clearing in which they stood. He wanted to stay in her light. To bask in her warmth and glow.

He'd never reacted to a woman this way before. They hadn't exchanged a hundred words, yet he wanted to drive her to the county courthouse in Elizabethtown and get a marriage license. Spend a week or two having a wedding night.

The heat must be getting to him. He usually maintained control in the face of adversity and disaster.

Wanting to marry a woman he'd met not five minutes ago qualified as a disaster. He didn't believe in love at first sight. Lust, maybe, and the stirring in his cock was undoubtedly lust. Indiscriminate sex could get a guy in trouble.

Darby Remington spelled trouble.

"Do you have a business card?" she asked. "In case I see anyone planting or cooking or even trespassing?"

The proper response would be to tell her to call 9-1-1. His ego—or maybe his dick—was flattered she wanted his number.

He pulled a business card from his shield wallet. "Call 9-1-1 first," he advised. There. He'd done the right thing. "I might be tied up collecting moose droppings or something."

They stood staring at each other until the crackle of the radio in his truck splintered the silence.

"I need to get back to work," he said.

"Me, too." She waved her notebook. "Lots to do. If I find any rogue deer ticks, I'll be sure to give you a call."

Chapter Two

Monday, June 12, 2000

Early the next morning, Ranger Winehouse walked into Chuck's Local Diner with another ranger. Darby's cheeks heated when she overheard his companion remark he couldn't believe Cam had never eaten there.

Where Darby worked wasn't a secret. Could he have asked around about her?

Regulars filled the booths. Tourists didn't frequent the Local. Chuck purposely kept the exterior looking as disreputable as village ordinances allowed. He hated dealing with what he called "the tourism counterculture. Only local culture at my counter." Then he'd guffaw.

Darby made a decent living waiting tables. Serving James Coolidge Astin had also led to inheriting Camp Nippletop.

"Good morning," Darby greeted the rangers as cheerfully as she could without sounding too eager. "No unruly bears wanting omelets this morning?"

Ranger Winehouse grinned at her, and her insides melted like butter on a stack hot off the griddle.

Darby had spent the night trying to purge the man from her head. From her dreams. Dangerous dreams. Stubborn male wouldn't budge. Now here he sat in the flesh. Well, in uniform. On duty.

The rangers claimed the last two stools at the counter, Sue Stone's jurisdiction. Darby didn't mind. His appearance so flustered her, she'd probably spill hot coffee in his lap.

Except Sue was the pretty waitress. Thin. Blond. Naturally vivacious, whereas drab Darby struggled with both her weight and her perkiness.

The last thing Darby needed was more rumors flying around the north country about her and her alleged lack of morals. She already figured in too much gossip. When word got out that Astin had left his historic Great Camp with an enormous trust fund to her, people had speculated about why chunky Darby Remington?

She'd been the first to wonder. Astin had been a regular at the diner. He always sat in one of her booths. Their relationship resembled that Jack Nicholson and Helen Hunt movie, *As Good As It Gets*—a cantankerous author and the waitress who endured his crap.

That was it. The full extent of their relationship. She hadn't realized Astin knew her last name.

Come to find out, only a few people knew he was a famous author, Darby being one. He'd won a Pulitzer or some other prestigious literary award. She'd read two of his books. The local library shelved them because he'd donated copies.

She'd once mentioned she enjoyed reading them.

He'd grumped at her.

She'd ignored his surliness and dropped more jelly packets on his table.

Then he'd died. Alone. Leaving her his property and the funds to transform the place into a writing retreat for other authors to bask in the solitude they needed to write. The camp he'd never wanted to share with anyone while he'd lived.

Death had made him generous.

Although Winehouse sat at the counter, Darby paid attention to his order. Eggs cooked sunny side up. Bacon. Orange juice. Whole wheat toast. Coffee, black. What a man ate for breakfast revealed a lot.

Even more revealing: he left a generous tip for Sue, a single mom, who could use the cash. Sue's baby daddy was a flake who was teaching their daughter a bunch of metaphysical nonsense. Darby personally thought the man inhaled too much incense.

On his way out the door, Ranger Winehouse touched his index and middle fingers to the visor of his hat in a friendly salute.

After her shift, Darby changed into jeans and a t-shirt and headed to Camp Nippletop. She planned to meet a contractor to discuss changes she wanted made to the main lodge, plus plans for rehabbing a few guest cabins.

The contractor beat her to the camp. At least, she thought the mud and rust encrusted truck belonged to the contractor. She couldn't tell where one element ended and the other began. The lack of a logo or other marking showing the company's name concerned her.

A scruffy-looking man with a heavy red beard stood on the porch. His steady stare as she parked her Jeep bothered her. She remembered Ranger Winehouse's warning about the escaped convict.

Maybe she ought to carry a gun if she were going to spend so much time alone in the forest.

"Hi," she greeted her visitor, as she climbed out of her Jeep. She waited for him to identify himself.

"You the new owner?"

No niceties from him.

"Yes. And you are?"

"A businessman who has a proposition for you."

Oh, that didn't sound good. She jammed her hand into her jeans pocket and slipped her keys between her fisted fingers as she inched back toward her Jeep.

"Heard you inherited old man Astin's place."

Damn gossips.

She swallowed hard. "Your point is?"

"I worked a deal with Astin. Rented land from him."

Darby didn't voice her skepticism. "I have my own plans for the property. In fact, I'm expecting my contractor at any minute."

The beard made reading the man's facial expression difficult. "He left. I told him you'd hired me. I don't want other people around while I'm doing business."

Her temper sparked. "You had no right."

"Sure I did. In case I haven't been clear, I'm going to lease land from you, and I don't want strangers snooping around."

Purchasing defense spray shot to the top of her to-do list. Ranger Winehouse had warned her. Maybe her dad would lend her his 12-gauge.

The sound of tires on the drive distracted her from forming a non-aggressive yet negative response to Red Beard's assertion.

"Shit," the man on the porch said, his tone vicious.

"Did I mention my fiancé might stop by?" Darby improvised. She waved at the yellow-striped, dark green truck, and prayed Ranger Winehouse was behind the wheel.

The driver parked the Department of Environmental Conservation vehicle next to her Jeep.

"Honey!" she called out, running toward the truck.

Ranger Winehouse climbed out.

"I'd hoped you'd drop in this afternoon." She threw herself at him and yanked his head down for a quick kiss.

Which turned out to be not so quick. Unless she lost time. Which she could have. He didn't resist, and in fact, had his tongue in her mouth and his hand on her bottom, squeezing one butt cheek as if he owned it.

He broke off the kiss but left his hand in place. "What's going on?" he murmured, as he nuzzled her ear.

"I thought he was a contractor. He's not." She slid her arm around Ranger Winehouse's waist. She'd worry about his marital status later. Right now, he belonged to her.

"Can I help you with something?" Winehouse asked the man on the porch, who appeared to be frozen. As if the scenario wasn't going the way he'd mentally scripted his encounter with the camp's new female owner.

"Ms. Remington and I got our signals crossed." Red Beard stomped off the porch and sauntered to his rust-pocked truck. "I'll be in touch."

"Oh, joy," she muttered.

As they watched the intruder leave, two things struck Darby. First, Red Beard knew her name, which scared the snot out of her. Second, Winehouse's arm clamped as firmly around her waist as hers wrapped around his.

She didn't want to let go, but she could be poaching another woman's territory.

"Thank goodness you showed up," she said, as she extracted herself. Reluctantly.

"You're trembling," Winehouse replied. "What's going on?"

"Sorry for throwing myself at you. He made me nervous," she babbled. "I need to buy defense spray."

"Not a bad idea, but you haven't answered my question. I suppose it's too much to hope that you couldn't resist my manly form." His teasing tone softened the sting of his words.

Embarrassment still burned in her face. Had she been too obvious? Being a full-figured girl didn't mean she was desperate.

"I needed to improvise. Making him believe a ranger stopped by regularly seemed like a good idea."

"It's a great idea," he replied in a soft voice, as if he didn't want her to hear. "Now, what did he want?"

"He wasn't the escaped prisoner?"

"The state troopers captured the prisoner early this morning in West Chazy. If you're going to keep deflecting my questions, I'm going to have to resort to illegal tactics."

Her imagination skittered to places it should not be going. He meant waterboarding or pulling out her fingernails, not stripping off her clothes, tying her to a bed, and having his wicked way with her. Unfortunately.

"What did you have in mind?" She clamped her hand across her mouth, not believing she'd asked the question aloud.

He responded with a slow grin. Teasing. Sexy.

She yanked off his sunglasses. Her breasts brushed against his chest. Her nipples tightened. She resisted the urge to cross her arms.

He stared into her eyes, not at her breasts. She'd previously noted his eyes were the same brown as the surface of an Adirondack lake. She now discovered deep seaweed-green spikes hidden in the depths. If she fell into his gaze, she would surely drown.

"Why don't I answer that over dinner tonight? But only if you tell me what's going on here. You were obviously frightened and relieved to see me." His tone shifted from flirtatious to serious.

Dinner? Like a date? That could end with another kiss? A real kiss, with more than his hand on her backside while she remained fully clothed? A fantasy come true. If he wasn't married or otherwise involved.

"He might be one of those marijuana farmers you warned me about." Darby related her dealings with Red Beard to Ranger Winehouse.

Cameron Winehouse had morphed into Mr. Law Enforcement. His teasing manner vanished. He was all business.

Relief filled Cam as he drove up to the camp and saw Darby. Her smile and waved greeting warmed him. When she'd called him "honey" and flung herself at him, demanding a kiss, he thought heaven had finally found him here on earth. He grabbed her ass and deepened the kiss without thinking.

Except part of him had been aware of the stranger on the porch. Instinct had warned him the rusty truck parked nose out meant trouble. Darby's trembling had temporarily superseded his ranger radar.

Now he was pissed. Pissed she hadn't told him right off about the stranger's implied threat. Pissed he'd been distracted by sex.

He hated his suspicion that Darby might be in cahoots with drug dealers. Especially when she danced around answering his questions. Yet her prevarications hadn't stopped him from flirting with her. He'd even asked her to dinner, his reason for visiting the camp again.

She studied her sneakered toe as she scuffed it into the dirt. Her cheeks were red. "You aren't married or anything, are you?"

It was a fair question. "No. Are you?"

"I mean, I shouldn't have kissed you. Especially if you're married or involved with someone."

"I'm glad you kissed me, and I'm not seeing anyone. Except, hopefully, you. We can discuss our future at dinner. Right now, tell me about your visitor."

"I'm not involved with him." She lifted her head and faced Cam. "I've never seen him before in my life. And I'll be honest. He scares me. He knows my name."

She wrapped her arms beneath her breasts, her magnificent breasts, as if hugging herself.

All his willpower focused on not replacing her arms with his. Crushing her against him. Holding her forever. It was too soon to stake his claim. "You shouldn't be out here alone."

She gave him a no-shit-Sherlock look. "I'd planned to meet the contractor. Red Beard sent him away."

Red Beard. As good a name as any.

"You didn't happen to get a look at his license plate, did you?" Cam had been too distracted to note the tag himself. Thinking with the wrong head.

Her eyebrows scrunched together, and her nose wrinkled. "I glanced at it when I got here because I didn't see a contractor sign on the truck door. Mud covered the plate."

Not surprising. Criminals frequently used mud to obscure a license plate.

"Except the nine at the beginning, like a dealer plate. I remember wondering what kind of dealer would put plates on a rust bucket." She laughed nervously. "Now I know. A drug dealer."

"You don't know for sure." Cam found little comfort in his own words.

"You're right. Except something about Red Beard bothered me. Not business-like at all, but more... militant. If that makes any sense. No buttering me up to get me to agree to lease land to him. He stated his demands and expectations of me as if I had no choice."

She shuddered. All expressions left her face. Her doe-wide eyes grew larger as she stared at him.

"What?"

"N-nothing," she stammered. "Just... I need to... to think some more."

"Would you mind if I poked around your property?" Her permission would keep things tidy in case he found something. He didn't have jurisdiction to search privately owned land unless he suspected a fire hazard. Meth labs were fire hazards, but rangers didn't go near them. Too dangerous. If they found evidence of one, they backed off and called in the state police.

She reacted as if his request surprised her. "No, of course not. I can show you—"

"You should go home," Cam interrupted. He didn't want her in the vicinity while he nosed around. He wanted her as far away from potential trouble as he could get her. "I'll pick you up at seven. If you agree to dinner."

"Don't you need my address?"

Why couldn't the woman simply say yes? *Yes, I'll have dinner with you. Yes, I will have mind-blowing sex with you. Yes, I will marry you and have your babies.* "I know where you live."

She stilled. "You do?"

Did she think he showed up for breakfast at the Local by accident? "Yes."

"Then I'm easy to find."

He hated how her voice warbled. He fought his first instinct to pull her close and kiss her, showing her he would protect her. "Hey. Don't worry. I have access to sources others don't, and my intentions are honorable. I came to ask you out face to face. You were busy at breakfast this morning."

"You don't worry me."

The tension in his chest eased. He reminded himself she was scared. He hadn't misread the passion in her embrace, in the way her mouth fit against his, and her response when he'd pulled her closer. Cam didn't indulge in imagination. He dealt in facts.

Point: Darby attracted him like no other woman.

Point: she'd kissed him first.

Point: Red Beard had frightened her.

Point: Cam could be an asshole and use her fear for his short-term gratification, or he could be himself and show her he could be trusted, and they were meant to spend the rest of their lives together.

Her enthusiastic *Honey, I'd hoped you'd drop in* gave him a glimpse of the future he wanted.

He needed to be cautious. "Can I have your cell phone number?" He'd been able to find only a land line for her.

"I don't have a cell phone. No signal most of the time."

Cam didn't agree with her logic. Yes, signals in the mountains were sporadic, but they were there. She needed a cell phone for emergencies. He'd buy her one later.

No one followed Darby home, much to her relief. Red Beard had shaken her more than she wanted to admit to herself, much less to the ranger.

She'd hoped he would kiss her again. He disappointed her.

Her telephone rang as she let herself into her apartment on the second floor of the Adirondack Bread and Cakes building. Cameron's name flashed in the caller ID window. Yeah, she'd programed in his number last night. Just in case. She was pathetic. "Hi," she answered.

"I wanted to make sure you got home okay."

She glanced around her compact space. "I'm fine." His concern pleased her.

"See you at seven." He disconnected.

She had a lot to do to get ready for their date.

Her regular days off were Tuesday and Wednesday. Staying out late wouldn't be an issue. Late? Try overnight.

Although cooking relaxed her, her refrigerator betrayed her tendency to eat at the diner. Soup, cereal, and frozen diet entrees comprised her usual shopping list. Today, she needed to plan for the best-case scenario, which involved serving Ranger Winehouse breakfast. Thanks to her vigilance that morning, she knew what he ate for breakfast.

And before providing breakfast? Condoms.

She needed to shop before she hit the shower and shaved her legs.

He didn't say where they were going for dinner, so she didn't know what to wear. Something red. She'd heard men liked the color red, and she desperately wanted Ranger Winehouse to like her. She rifled through her closet and debated shopping for a new outfit. Not that she had time to browse even Saranac Lake's limited options.

Oh. No need to bother, because in the back of her closet, where she'd forgotten she'd put it, hung the perfect dress.

Cam battled black flies and mosquitos as he hiked to the more remote parts of Darby's Nippletop property. He didn't like what he found. He radioed in his suspicions about Camp Nippletop being used as an illegal grow-site. No signs of a meth lab, though. Dopers were the province of the state police, not the DEC. His supervisor would pass along the information to the troopers. Cam also gave a sketchy description of Red Beard's truck—make and model, mud-spattered dealer plates.

He also made sure not to implicate Darby, to emphasize she'd given him permission to explore her property.

Cam had barely enough time to drive home and shower. He debated shaving. Women, he'd heard, liked the scruffy-bearded look. His stubble wouldn't be at the so-called sexy stage until tomorrow night. Maybe Darby wouldn't notice.

He replaced the condoms in his wallet with three new ones. He couldn't remember the last time he'd restocked and didn't want to take any chances with birth control failure. Yes, he wanted Darby to bear his children, but he didn't want her to feel forced into marrying him because of an unplanned pregnancy.

He arrived at her place several minutes before seven. He parked around the corner.

A chill freshened the air as he approached her door, although the sun wouldn't set for another hour and a half. Nineteenth century business magnates had built their summer homes in the Adirondacks for a reason. The mountains offered a cool, clean escape from filthy, scorching cities.

Adirondack-born and bred, being a forest ranger had been Cam's goal ever since he could remember. How many men could claim they were living their dream?

Now he was about to spend time with his fantasy woman. Life didn't get much better.

He jabbed the pushbutton next to her door, before calling her phone. "It's Cam Winehouse," he said when she answered. "I'm downstairs."

"I'll be right down."

She ought to have an intercom to check visitors' identities.

He studied the flimsy lock as he listened to her footsteps descending an interior staircase. Then he heard the slide of a safety chain before she opened the door. A safety chain never stopped anyone who wanted entrance. Neither would the sorry excuse for a deadbolt lock.

When she opened the door, her fragrance banished all thought. She smelled like cinnamon rolls. Or maybe the aroma originated from the bakery on the ground floor.

Her appearance stole his breath. A red polka-dotted dress clung to her lust-inducing breasts like a second skin. He didn't see a single bra line—and he searched. He calculated how many of the big white buttons marching down the front of the dress he'd have to undo before the fabric fell away.

His cock stirred inside his chinos.

Her full skirt flirted with her knees as she turned and locked the deadbolt with her key. She gave the handle a tug to check its security. Silver sandals, which exposed her red-painted toenails, twinkled in the sun.

If not for the locked door and flight of stairs between her and her bed, he might have tossed her over his shoulder and carried her upstairs to fuck her blind.

She draped a length of red fabric across her shoulders in deference to the chill. "You didn't say where we were going."

As if she needed an excuse to be beautiful.

Cam cupped her elbow and steered her toward his vehicle. "I thought we'd try the new steak place outside Lake Placid. Unless you don't eat meat."

Damn. He should have checked her preferences before he'd made the reservations.

"Oh, I'm a carnivore." Her red lips curved. "Glad to learn you are, too. One question. Are you Ranger Winehouse or Cameron tonight?"

He couldn't tell if she was blushing or if the sun reflecting the color of her dress tinted her face.

"I'm Cam. All the time for you." He blipped off the locks on his vehicle. "Except when you call me *honey*." It felt as if gravel filled his throat when he spoke.

"Sorry," she muttered.

He opened the passenger door for her. "Why? I liked it."

Chapter Three

Dim lights barely illuminated the restaurant. Heavy white linen tablecloths and napkins graced the tables. Muted instrumental music played in the background. Darby had never eaten in such an elegant place. She was glad she'd worn a dress.

"I'm going to have a beer," Cam said, as he handed the tasseled wine list to her. "If you want something else, please order it."

Relieved, she handed the folder back to him without opening it. "I prefer beer, too."

"Two Moonsingers," he told their server.

After getting over her shock at the menu prices, she told Cam what she wanted... to eat... at the restaurant. She needed to get her mind out of the gutter... bed. Needed to be in the moment with him, not fantasizing about what might come... er, happen.

Every thought morphed into a double entendre.

She focused on the restaurant, taking mental notes of what she found comfortable and what she did not. She could never work in such a fancy, overdone establishment unless someone shoved a long stick up her butt.

He raised his pilsner glass—no bottles or cans at the tables here. "To… us." His gaze seemed to pin her in place.

Something in her chest—besides her nipples—tightened as she tapped her glass against his. "Us," she repeated. She sipped her beer. Not bad. She usually drank Molson Golden, but the Moonsinger would do.

He smiled at her. His rusty-brown eyes were bright. Interested. "How did you end up with the Great Camp?"

Heat infused her cheeks. *Not again.* Trying to convince people she'd done nothing to or with Astin to warrant suspicion frustrated her. She'd been shocked when Howard Chatham contacted her about the inheritance.

"James Coolidge Astin was a breakfast regular at the diner. He always sat in one of my booths, even though Chuck tried to get him to sit at the counter so the booth could be used for more customers. I defended him. He was grumpy enough as it was. I shudder to think how nasty he would have been if Chuck had forced the issue." She shredded the damp corner of the cocktail napkin the server had provided with her beer. Talking about her non-relationship with Astin always bothered her. "I happened to find a book in the library written by someone with the same name, so I asked him about it. That's how I found out he was an author. He acted put out, but I think he was pleased when I read a second book of his. That's it."

"You're an example of why people should be kind to others," he said when she finished.

His response confused her. Everyone else, including her family, condemned her. Many people accused her of trading sexual favors in order to get her hands on the land. As if she'd ever traded sex for anything in her life.

Hopefully, she could update her status later tonight.

"Well, I'm not sure it's all good," she confessed. "Mr. Astin specified definite ideas about how the retreat is to be run. No internet. No cable television. He wanted cell phone jammers, but—"

"They're illegal in the US."

"Yeah." Darby wrinkled her nose. "It's not as though cell phone signals are reliable around his property."

"Your property," Cam reminded her.

The server interrupted with their salads, a breadbasket, and the story behind the artisan rolls being offered.

When they were alone again, Darby asked Cam why he'd become a forest ranger. Anything to stop talking about Astin's will. She needed a break from worrying about a project she feared was too big for her to handle.

Besides, the man sitting across from her intrigued her.

Cam obliged her. Passion for his profession animated his features. His Adirondack roots rivaled hers.

Everything about him thrilled her. He wore his coffee-brown hair cut close to his head. She admired his thick fingers as he lifted his glass to his mouth. An indent in the center of his chin begged to be explored by her tongue. Dark curls peeked at her from the open vee of his button-down shirt. He'd rolled back his sleeves to his elbows, exposing muscles, more dark hair, and a tattoo on the inside of his left forearm. Other tatts on his biceps teased her every time he moved his arms. Her libido kicked into overdrive.

Could Darby Remington get any more perfect? She listened intently while he blathered on about being a forest ranger, sipped beer instead of wine, and enjoyed her steak. Her Adirondack roots were as old and deep as his.

Not to mention how the top button on her dress nestling in the deep shadow of her cleavage tantalized him.

Neither wanted after-dinner coffee or dessert. He figured the Mountain Mist Custard stand in Saranac Lake would still be open. They could eat soft-serve ice cream on the deck and watch the setting sun reflect on the Saranac River. Maybe an invitation for coffee in her apartment would follow. And after? Well, a man could hope.

He was a man.

He paid the check, then helped Darby drape her pretty wrap across her shoulders.

The comfortable silence between them as he drove toward Saranac Lake pleased him. Darby didn't chatter, filling every gap in conversation with inanities.

Cam appreciated the quiet. The solitude of being a ranger suited him. Listening to the breeze cavorting in the trees fulfilled him. Mostly, he enjoyed living alone, too, until Darby tempted him with what he'd been missing.

Ending the evening with frozen custard alongside the river turned out to be a popular idea. A crowd mobbed Mountain Mist. Watercraft bobbed at the dock behind the stand and vehicles filled the parking lot.

"I couldn't eat another bite," Darby assured him.

Cam briefly considered heading to his place. They could sit on his deck and enjoy the stars twinkling in the night sky like a woman's fancy party dress. Except he'd be better off at her apartment in case he needed to leave because the night didn't end the way he hoped.

Thanks to the pub on the corner, no open spaces remained at the curb near the bakery.

He didn't see her Jeep. "Where do you park?"

"A small lot behind the bakery." She hesitated. "Three spaces. I get one. The others are for the owner and an employee. They usually arrive around five in the morning."

Cam waited.

"Would you like to come up for coffee?"

She sounded as tentative as he felt.

He glanced at her profile, half-hidden by shifting shadows as he slowly circled the block. A woman didn't invite a man in unless she didn't want the evening to end. When did she expect him to leave?

He tested the waters. "As long as I'm out by five?"

Instead of answering, she pointed to taillights angling away from the curb. "Someone is pulling out between the white van and dark pickup."

Her enthusiasm gave him hope.

They didn't speak as they strolled to her apartment. He wanted to say many things, but they could wait. He'd rather show her.

Darby pulled her wrap closer. Cam considered draping his arm across her shoulders, except he was afraid to touch her. Afraid he would never let her go. Afraid his basic need for her might be moving too fast.

They stopped in front of her door. She clutched her key.

"Let me." He took the key from her. His mother had raised him right.

The door gaped open. Not wide, but not closed, much less secured. He distinctly recalled Darby locking, then checking the door before they left for dinner. The hair on his nape rippled. He wished he'd carried his side arm, instead of securing his Sig Sauer in the gun safe at home.

"Do you have a roommate?" he asked.

"No."

"Does anyone else have a key to your place?" *Your BFF from high school? An old boyfriend? A current lover?*

Her eyes were as wide as a frightened deer's. "Only my landlord."

Twilight stained the sky. A bank of old-fashioned lights above the bakery window illuminated not only a display of fancy cupcakes but also a portion of the sidewalk. People were out and about, crawling between the pubs and pizzerias scattered along the main thoroughfare. Yet someone had picked Darby's lock without being noticed.

Red Beard. If the man used Camp Nippletop to grow illegal crops, he posed a danger to Darby.

Cam put his hand on Darby's waist and nudged her into the bakery's recessed doorway before pulling out his cellphone and poking at the number pad. The Village of Saranac Lake fielded its own police department.

"What now?" Darby whispered.

"I'm calling 9-1-1," Cam replied.

CHAPTER FOUR

MONDAY, JUNE 12, 2000 CONTINUED

So much for her plan to seduce the sexy forest ranger. Darby pulled her shawl closer and crossed her arms over her breasts. Cam spoke to the lone officer who'd responded to the call, then rejoined Darby as the officer mounted the stairs.

Cam put his arm around her, immediately warming her. "Are you okay?"

"This isn't how I imagined the evening ending," she muttered.

"The night is still young." He gave her a quick squeeze.

Young only because the next two days were her regularly scheduled days off. Her six-in-the-morning-to-three-in-the-afternoon shift at the Local generally had her in bed by nine.

Darby didn't want to remind Cam she worked in the pink-collar world. Many people ignored waitstaff and other service industry employees. Not her. After she had Astin's writing refuge up and running, she would treat the staff like gods and goddesses. She would be one of the best employers in the High Peaks.

Not that she could compete with places like Lake Placid's Mirror Lake Inn or the Sagamore Resort in Lake George. But then her clientele wouldn't believe the chips on their shoulders were diamonds, either.

"Maybe I forgot to lock the door," she ventured. "I'm going to feel silly when the police don't find anything."

"You locked it. You double checked it. I remember admiring you for your thoroughness."

She basked in his praise. She always tested the lock. Not that she owned anything valuable. But the shabby flat above the bakery was her space. That someone had broken in and touched her belongings felt as violating as if the person had attacked her body.

Exactly like Red Beard's appearance on the Great Camp porch.

Red Beard knew her name. Knew when she would be at Camp Nippletop. It stood to reason he also knew where she lived.

She shuddered, and Cam tightened his embrace. "Would you rather wait in my car? I can turn on the heat."

She didn't want to confess she shivered from fright, not cold. "I'm a north country girl. I'll be fine."

"You're wearing a Miami Beach dress." He'd worked a hand under her shawl. His calloused palm cupped her bare shoulder, his thumb rubbing a circle into her skin. "Let me warm you,"

Darby wrestled an urge to bury her face in his shirtfront and weep. She never cried, so the impulse confused her. Fear usually triggered anger in her, not girly-girl behavior.

"We could always go to my place." His voice created a deep rumble in his chest.

Her lungs stuttered.

The sound of footfalls on the stairs leading from her apartment saved her from replying. When the police officer emerged from her front door, the bakery's display lights glinted off his name badge. Officer Ellis.

"Well?" Cam asked as he positioned himself in front of Darby.

Cam taking charge confused her. She paid the rent and lived there.

"Your burglar is gone. It appears someone broke in the back door—they smashed the lock—and exited through the front. I may have found something... out of place and need you to confirm." Officer Ellis shot Cam a look Darby couldn't interpret. "Also, you'll need to see if anything is missing. I'll escort you upstairs."

"Earlier today, a possible grower approached her." Cam's clipped tone sounded as precise as an official report.

"I inherited property in St. Huberts," Darby hastened to explain. "A man showed up wanting to lease some land. He told me he'd worked out an agreement with the previous owner. I don't know if he planned to do anything illegal. He made me nervous."

"He took off damn fast when I arrived," Cam interjected. "I'm a forest ranger."

Ellis acknowledged Cam's statement with a nod. "I thought you looked familiar. Let's go upstairs and look around."

Cam kept his hand on the base of Darby's back as she followed Ellis. The tension in her body reminded him of a fishing pole with a ten-pound large-mouth bass fighting the hook. The line could snap at any minute. He would provide a safety net and catch her.

Darby's cozy apartment resembled one of his great-grandmother's handmade patchwork quilts, crazy with patterns and colors. He trailed Darby as Officer Ellis ushered her through the rooms. Sitting room, kitchen, no-space-to-move bathroom, to the scene where he'd hoped to —

Darby gasped and fled the bedroom.

Ellis muttered something unintelligible.

Torn between needing to comfort her and wanting to see what upset her, Cam followed Darby into the kitchen.

She stood with her arms braced on the counter, head bowed, and her back to the room. Her hunched shoulders weren't shaking, so he didn't think she was crying.

"Hey," he said, as he approached her. He didn't want to startle her. He lightly rested his palms on her shoulders.

She straightened her spine. Turned to face him.

"What upset you?"

"The knife."

"Where?" He gently massaged her soft skin. He hadn't seen a knife.

"This is so embarrassing." Her voice hitched.

He rubbed his hands along her arms. "You can tell me. No judgment here."

She gestured toward a knife block on the counter. All the slots were in use except one. "The intruder took a steak knife and stabbed some... items on my nightstand."

"What items?"

She wouldn't look at him. The color flooding her cheeks matched her dress.

He released her and sought her bedroom to see for himself. The knife stood visibly upright. He inched closer.

"Don't touch anything," Officer Ellis warned.

As if Cam didn't understand crime scene procedures. He merely wanted to see why Darby acted so weirdly.

Condoms. The knife skewered a stack of rubbers.

Whoa. He swallowed hard.

While he couldn't help but like that she'd been prepared to be intimate with him, he recognized the threat. His reasons for taking her to his place doubled. She needed protection and damaged birth control wasn't the only danger.

Officer Ellis interrupted his musings. "I've called the state police crime scene unit. "

"Good," Cam said, as he hurried to rejoin Darby in the kitchen.

She'd regained her composure in his absence, although her cheeks were still pink. She clutched a long strip of paper in her hand.

"Here's the thing." Her voice cracked as she lifted her chin. "I'd planned to offer you breakfast."

Darby twisted the cash register tape from her afternoon purchases. She'd found the receipt on the table and grabbed it before anyone else could see it. Now she clung to the paper as a lifeline. She needed something to do with her hands.

Cam's eyes appeared to glow. "I'd hoped you would."

He spoke so softly she barely heard him.

Nerves made her babble. She waved the receipt. "I bought bacon and eggs. I noticed that's what you ordered at the Local."

"Let me see." He gently pulled the receipt from her grasp, and continued speaking in a teasing tone, as if calming her was the only thing that mattered. He probably did the same for stranded hikers. "Need to make sure you're not going to poison me."

Oh no!

She tried to snatch the paper back.

Too late.

"Orange juice and butter, too," he murmured as he read.

Darby knew exactly what he was reading when his eyebrows arched. The blood vessels in her face were ready to burst.

"*Thirty-six* condoms? Should I be flattered or insulted?"

She wanted to duck her head. Not meet his gaze. Crawl away in humiliation.

Oh heck, she was an adult. She could have sex with anyone she wanted to. Condoms were good. Condoms meant safe sex. Why should wanting protection embarrass her?

Unless Cam didn't want to have sex with her, but she didn't think she'd misinterpreted the situation. They'd been exchanging signals all night. He'd fondled her butt that afternoon. Then again, she could be misreading everything. She wasn't an expert on seducing a guy or the type of woman to whom men flocked.

Maybe she was crazy, but Cameron Winehouse heated her insides the way no other man had. She'd have to brazen out the rest of her imagined scenario.

She lifted her chin. "Given the circumstances, I'm glad I'm an optimist."

"Hey." He dropped the receipt on the table and closed the distance between them. He lowered his voice. "No worries. We're on the same page. I came prepared, too."

Darby's breath hitched. He was going to kiss her. He was going to put his hands on her hips, draw her close and —

"I need you to answer a few questions for my report," Officer Ellis said as he strode into the kitchen. "While we wait for the troopers."

"Of course," Darby squeaked out as Cam took several steps back. "Let's sit at the table. Except I only have the two chairs."

"I'm good." Cam leaned against the counter.

Every molecule in her body sensed how his eyes fixed on her. He focused on her, his intensity comforting her instead of creeping her out. He made her feel safe.

Ellis joined Darby at the table. "Other than the guy this afternoon, do you have any idea who might have broken in? Maybe an old boyfriend who's upset you're seeing someone else?"

"No," Darby replied. Her last boyfriend had been in second grade. "No one. I don't do relationships."

Cam straightened. What the hell did she mean, *I don't do relationships*? The statement could explain the economy-size box of condoms. He and Darby needed to have a serious discussion before the need-a-rubber stage.

Ellis asked other questions. Darby answered. Cam remained silent until she mentioned Red Beard.

"He made me nervous." Darby twisted her fingers. "I didn't pay much attention to details."

"You sensed something about him was off, and you noticed the license plate," Cam corrected her. "You did everything right."

"Only that the tag started with nine. My cousin told me that means it's a dealer plate. Mud covered everything else."

"Not uncommon with growers," Ellis muttered.

"I poked around a bit but didn't find anything illegal. Growing season doesn't begin until next month, so I'm not surprised. I've alerted the state police," Cam said.

"I don't know if Red Beard is a criminal," Darby insisted. "He didn't say he planned to grow illegal drugs, cook meth, or form his own army, only that he said he wanted to lease some land. He made me uncomfortable."

She squeezed her eyes shut. Tears glistened in the corners but didn't fall, not even after she opened them again.

"He knows my name." Her voice cracked. "He knows I inherited Camp Nippletop, and *he knows my name*."

The panic in her voice sealed the deal for Cam. He wasn't going to let her out of his sight. She would have to reconsider her stance on relationships.

"Your inheritance isn't a secret." Ellis's tone lost its professional polish. "People question why Old Man Astin left all that land and money to you. You have to admit it's odd."

Darby's jaw jutted. Her eyes sparked. Anger vibrated off her, quickly replacing the fear. "Are you accusing me of something? Are you saying I'm *asking* for trouble? *Are you blaming me for being a victim*?"

Cam wanted to punch Ellis in the mouth for the insinuation, but Darby defended her herself without his help.

Ellis looked flustered before his cop face snapped into place. "Not at all. I made a statement about a situation which might have bearing on the break-in."

"You were out of line, making a personal observation," Darby corrected. "Stick to the facts. I don't need speculation or attitude."

Cam's admiration for her increased several notches.

Ellis cleared his throat. "Can you describe the trespasser?"

"A bushy red beard hid most of his face. All he needs to do is shave, and I wouldn't recognize him if he stood on my porch again," Darby admitted.

Cam agreed but added: "His beard would have taken a while to grow. I doubt he'll shave anytime soon."

"Except it's distinctive," Darby pointed out. "We can ID him using it."

"The troopers will check if any merchants in the area have video surveillance," Ellis said. "If your trespasser is behind the break-in, and he is a grower, you don't want to fool around with him."

Darby stayed in the kitchen and let Cam deal with the two state troopers who'd responded to Ellis's call. She busied herself making coffee. Measuring water in the carafe with shaking hands. Pouring it into the reservoir without splashing her dress. Fitting the filter into the basket. Pulling the Folgers from the freezer. The burst of aroma as she removed the plastic lid from the cold metal container made her long for her usual mundane existence.

"Hey there." Cam snuck up behind her.

Darby jumped. No, he hadn't snuck. She'd been so preoccupied she hadn't heard him. She tried to smile. Didn't happen. "I'm making coffee." Spoken as if he couldn't see her measuring the grounds into the basket.

Facing Cam after he'd seen the steak knife jammed into the condoms she'd left on her night table still embarrassed her. Could she have made her expectation for the night to end with sex any clearer?

"The guys will like that," Cam said.

Like what? Sex? No. *Coffee.* They were discussing coffee.

"You should pack a bag. You can't stay here." Cam's intense gaze bored through her. "Someone smashed your locks. You're not safe."

What did he mean, *pack a bag*? Was he inviting her to his place? Even the meanest motel room in the resort area was beyond her budget. She couldn't stay at the Great Camp, since Red Beard proved he could get to her there, but her parents in Wilmington would welcome her.

She opened the cupboard where she kept the collection of her family's cast-off mugs.

"Let me get those." Cam's height could better reach the upper shelves. He stood behind her. Close, yet not touching. Caging her against the counter. Ignoring the cupboard. "We need to have a serious conversation," he said, his voice a low rumble against her ear.

His large hand hovered near her cheek, as if he wanted to cradle it, but was afraid to touch her.

"Offering me breakfast was your thing. Here's mine."

She strained to hear his soft voice.

"You may not do relationships, but I don't do casual sex."

Her stomach plummeted. She ought to be used to rejection. She'd taken a chance and failed.

"If we start something," he continued, "we're exclusive."

Although Cam couldn't see Darby's face, her body language spoke volumes. He'd laid it on the line for her. She was everything he ever wanted, and he didn't share. He would prove to her how good intimacy between them could be. She was the one. His one. She wouldn't need anyone other than him.

She'd stiffened when he said he didn't do casual sex, then jerked her head once and answered in a hoarse voice. "Exclusive. No problem."

He closed his fingers into his palm and traced the line of her cheek with a knuckle. Her skin was soft. So soft. He spoke against her ear. "Good. You also need to know I enjoy foreplay. A lot."

She swallowed hard enough for the ripple of her throat muscles to travel to her face.

"Including kissing." He opened his fist and let his fingers tangle in the curls brushing her shoulders. "Especially kissing."

She faced him, her mouth tilted toward his. He lowered his head. Their lips brushed.

He clamped down on his need to consume her. Possess her. Going too fast would scare her. He needed to know if she felt the same about him. She'd bought condoms, which was a good sign they were headed in the direction he wanted.

"Anything else?" She, too, whispered.

He dropped his hand from her shoulder to her waist, bypassing the tantalizing white buttons holding the front of her dress together. He pulled her as close as he dared. "I can't wait to find out if you're as soft all over as you look."

Darby thought she was melting from the inside out as Cam's tongue probed her mouth. He didn't seem to mind her fullness. Big boobs, big butt—yeah, soft was one way to describe her body. She thought about the things she ought to share with him—okay, one thing—but possibly an important thing. He'd told her his... expectations. She ought to reciprocate. Except she didn't want to scare him off. Or guilt him into behaving differently. She didn't want caution on his part. She wanted him. From the moment he'd climbed out of his truck—only yesterday—she'd wanted him to be the one to whom she could give her virginity.

Someone cleared his throat. Darby jerked. She'd forgotten they weren't alone. Cam's caresses drove away all rationality. And she must do the same to him because he'd firmly planted his hands on her backside. She peered around Cam. Yep. A red-faced trooper stood in the kitchen doorway, staring at her ceiling.

"I made coffee. If you're interested." Darby extracted herself from Cam's clutches and aimed for her perky-waitress-voice. She figured she fell short because the tightness in her throat barely allowed basic speech. She couldn't speak for the red-faced trooper, but she could brew coffee on her cheeks. "Cam, can you get down the mugs?"

The task would keep his back to the room. Unless he wanted to wave his erection around like a man-signal, proving he'd marked his territory.

She ducked beneath Cam's arm. "Cream and sugar coming up."

"That would be great, thanks," the trooper responded. He still wouldn't look at Darby, instead focusing so intently on the window, he might have been measuring for new curtains. "We're nearly done here. I do have a few questions."

"No, I don't have a jealous ex," Darby said before he could ask. She understood why the cops believed a knife stabbed through condoms screamed a past relationship gone bad, but they didn't know her. She placed the sugar and milk on the counter near the coffeepot.

"Could someone else object to your relationship with Ranger Winehouse?"

"Not that I'm aware." Nor did she have a relationship with Ranger Winehouse. Yet. "What about you, Cam? Any possessive former girl-friends?"

He turned. A quick glance below his belt confirmed he'd calmed his body. "Nope. My last relationship ended a year ago, and she's the one who ended it."

"She didn't expect you to come running after her?" the trooper asked.

"We weren't that serious."

"No groupies? Women with a forest ranger fetish?" the trooper pressed.

Cam leveled his glare at the man. "No."

"Did Officer Ellis tell you we suspect a possible dope grower?" Darby interjected.

"He's the reason we were called in," the trooper replied. "We have Ellis's report, but why don't you tell me about your encounter."

So Darby retold her tale as she served coffee all around. Cam confirmed her recitation with his own observations.

The trooper didn't ask additional questions. He drained his mug and stood. "Thanks for the coffee, Ms. Remington. You might want to find someplace else to stay tonight. The intruder damaged your locks."

Vertigo washed through her. Her embarrassment at being caught having her butt groped displaced her fear for a while. The trooper's reminder brought the panic back with a vengeance.

She needed her notebook. *Call landlord regarding locks.* Making a list would give her a sense of control.

"Thanks," Cam said, as he escorted the troopers and Ellis to the door.

A moment later, she and Cam were alone.

"As much as I like your dress," he said, as he traced the top button with his forefinger, "you should change into something more comfortable before we head out."

"I hate to sound stupid," Darby replied, her pulse racing. "I also don't want to assume anything. What do you have in mind?"

He toyed with the button. His fingertips brushed the skin at the top of her breasts. His hands were warm, but the heat didn't prevent her nipples from crinkling as if they'd been hit by an Arctic blast.

"I have a place in Ray Brook. We could sit on the deck. The sky is pretty this time of year. Not as impressive as the Perseids meteor showers in August, but stargazing is my favorite way to relax after a stressful day. You're stressed."

"Okay." Her insides sagged in relief.

"We can explore other relaxation methods, too." He slipped the white plastic disk through the buttonhole. Slid several fingers into the gap and stroked the top slope of her left breast. "You should change. Pack clothes for tomorrow. Oh, and bring your important paperwork. You wouldn't want your identity stolen."

"What?" His touch befuddled her. Again.

"Your Social Security card. Birth certificate. Passport, if you have one. Your copy of Astin's will. Papers like that. Identity theft is real, and you own some extremely valuable property. Besides, you never know when you might need them."

Chapter Five

Cam washed the mugs and coffee carafe while he waited for Darby to change and pack. Keeping busy meant he wouldn't do something stupid, like ask her if she wanted to elope.

She reappeared as he unplugged the coffee maker as a safety precaution. Although he approved of her snug jeans, dark green hooded sweatshirt, and sneakers, he preferred the red polka-dotted dress with the big white buttons.

She carried a Paul Smith's College duffel and her purse.

"I'm going to follow you in my Jeep," she said.

He opened his mouth to argue.

She didn't pause long enough for him to speak. "I don't have to work tomorrow, but I have errands to do. Plans. I don't want to inconvenience you."

"If you plan to go to the camp by yourself... I wish you wouldn't." As much as he wanted to tell her what to do, he couldn't. He could only make suggestions and hope she'd see reason.

She pursed her lips. "No choice. But first, I'm buying pepper spray."

He'd have to get her one of the larger cans of oleoresin capsicum spray issued to law enforcement, at least until they'd resolved the situation with Red Beard. Until that happened, he didn't want to let her out of his sight. "I'll go with you. You're not the only one who has a day off."

"You planned our evening well. Wait. That didn't come out right. I know you didn't arrange the break-in, but—"

"You kissed me." He didn't know how else to explain without scaring her off. She didn't strike him as being skittish. He liked her nerve. That and her practicality.

"You kissed me back," she pointed out.

"Yes, I did. And I'd like to kiss you again." *Every day for the rest of my life.*

"Good." Her grin was shaky. "What are we waiting for?"

Cam accompanied Darby to her Jeep, for which she was grateful. The poorly lit parking lot behind the bakery had never bothered her before. He checked her vehicle, too. Tires intact? Yes. Lurkers in the backseat? No.

She drove him to where he'd parked his SUV, then followed him out of the village on a highway that slithered and coiled through the dark forest like a serpent.

Thank goodness she wouldn't be alone, not after the break-in at her apartment. She hated being afraid, and she would have been too scared to sleep in her own bed.

She admitted to being anxious, though. A smidge. Not because of Cam. He was the best part of the whole mess. His calm. His support. No, her inexperience and the awkwardness of the situation caused her trepidation.

Situation? Call it what it is. Sex.

Her attraction to Cam relieved her. She'd sometimes questioned why she didn't want to shed her clothes whenever a guy kissed her or tried to touch her. Sex came naturally to most other people, but never to her.

She squirmed in her seat as the unfamiliar sensations insisted on making themselves known and prayed she wouldn't make a fool of herself.

Using Cam's taillights as a beacon, she followed as he pulled onto a side road. A mile or so later, he entered a driveway canopied by towering pines. She parked next to him. Her hands were sweaty on the steering wheel, her mouth was dry, and her heart careened in her chest. Maybe he wouldn't notice anything amiss. She could improvise being experienced. Waitressing required putting on a false face.

Cam opened her vehicle door but didn't touch her, not even brushing against her hand as he took her duffel from her. Nor did he speak except to warn her to watch her step. Cool moonlight filtered through the overhead branches but did nothing to squelch the heat flickering in every cell in her body. She feared she would spontaneously combust while she waited for him to unlock his door.

Once inside, she stopped, not sure what to do. Dense shadows blinded her and smelled like the forest surrounding them. She heard something drop to the floor a split second before Cam pulled her close and covered her mouth with his. The taste of coffee lingered in his mouth. The urgency he'd shown in her apartment intensified a thousand-fold. His heat ignited everything smoldering inside her.

She wrapped her arms around him with unspoken permission to do whatever he wanted, signaling she trusted him with body, heart, and soul.

He broke off the kiss long enough to say in a low growl, "I thought I could wait, but I can't." He nipped, then sucked on her earlobe between whispering rash, irrational vows as he danced her through the darkness.

She vowed to hold him to each one of those promises.

Shivers skittered along every one of her neural pathways. Instead of landing in her brain, they congregated lower. Between her upper thighs. Her girl bits had become the center of her universe. She finally understood why sex made women stupid. She would do anything to relieve the pressure, the incessant craving swamping her senses.

Cam tugged at her sweatshirt as he nuzzled her neck.

Something hit the back of her thighs. The next thing she knew, she lay flat on a mattress, her breasts exposed.

Thank goodness she hadn't bothered with a bra.

"We're wearing too many clothes," Cam murmured, as he yanked the sweatshirt over her head. He sucked a nipple into his magical mouth while struggling with the brass button at her waist.

"You're right." Her voice creaked. She reached for him, inhaling deeply, to mingle his scent with her essence.

No grace softened their contortions, no beauty of movement as sneakers and boots clunked to the floor. Frantic need consumed her as she explored his chest with her mouth and hands. Lips and fingers memorized the shapes and textures of his muscles so she would always recognize them, recognize him, no matter how dark the night.

"I changed my mind." Cam buried his face between her breasts. "I'm not going to last, not this time. I will make everything up to you, I swear, but right now if I don't—"

"Yes. Please."

She squirmed against the hand he'd burrowed between her thighs. Judging by her slickness, her eagerness matched his.

He rolled away and groped for his discarded pants. His wallet. A condom. Another time, he might have invited her to help. Not tonight.

Once covered, he settled himself between her splayed legs. He needed to be inside her more than he'd ever needed anything in his life. He would correct any shortcomings or failures another time. The rest of their lives. "I need you so much," he muttered against her ear.

He thrust.

Darby gasped and stiffened.

What the—?

Tight. Too tight. He couldn't wrap his head around what his dick signaled to him. He wasn't *that* big. All his willpower focused on not moving. Not hurting her any more than he already had.

"Don't stop." She looped her arms under his. Dug her fingers into his shoulders. Locked her ankles at the base of his back. Wiggled her hips. "Please don't stop."

Darby kissed Cam to keep him from saying anything. Shimmied her butt to remind him to move. Yeah, penetration stung, but she figured the discomfort would go away.

Cam jerked his head out of her grasp. The intensity with which he stared at her might have frightened a lesser woman.

Darby knew what she wanted, and she wanted Cam Winehouse.

"You promised," she reminded him.

He hesitated another moment before fulfilling his promise.

And later, only a few minutes later, when she was boneless and weak and struggling for air, with his heart thudding against her breasts as heavily as his body weighed her to the mattress, she wondered how soon they could do it again.

He groaned and rolled off her. "Don't you move," he ordered, as he lurched to his feet. He snapped on the bedside lamp before staggering out of the room.

Where did he think she'd go? Even if her muscles cooperated—and she would bet her inheritance they wouldn't—she had no place to run.

"Sit up," he commanded in a rough voice when he returned. She did.

He clamped a hot, wet washcloth against her girl bits.

"Oh. That feels good." She smiled at him.

"Is there anything you want to tell me?"

He stared into her eyes, like a silent movie portrayal of a hypnotist mesmerizing a victim. Except she refused to be a victim.

"I really enjoyed myself."

He brushed a lock of hair off her cheek. "I meant the thing you forgot to mention."

"I didn't forget. You misunderstood what I told the trooper about not doing relationships."

"I thought you meant you only did one-night stands."

His comment should have been insulting, but she understood his confusion.

"Why didn't you warn me?" he continued. "I would have taken more time to prepare you. Been more careful."

"I didn't want you to be careful. I wanted you loony with lust. Like me. I wanted you to act as if we've been lovers for weeks. Months. Years."

Cam's dark eyes searched her face, as if looking for a lie. "You didn't give me a chance to make your first time something special."

He sounded so sincere he nearly broke Darby's heart. She placed her palms on his rock-hard shoulders. As much as she wanted to explore the swirls of black ink decorating his skin, she could wait. Cam's vulnerability—although he would never admit to being insecure—needed reassurance.

"I was feeling instead of thinking. You do that to me, you know. No one else has ever come close. When you got out of your truck yesterday, I almost swooned."

"Swooned?" He made a sound she interpreted as a snort.

"Okay, maybe not swooned. Attacked you. Like I did this afternoon because Red Beard gave me an excuse. Then you asked me out, and I ran to the drugstore to buy condoms."

"I cheated you. You gave me a gift, and I tore into it because I didn't know."

That might have been the sweetest thing anyone had ever said to her.

"Then you're just going to have to make it up to me."

Chapter Six

Monday, June 12–Tuesday, June 13, 2000

Two condoms later, Cam suggested they get dressed to avoid being devoured by insects while sitting on the deck. En route, he grabbed a couple of bottles of Moonsinger from the fridge. It was late, well past his usual bedtime, but he wanted to share his slice of the Adirondacks with Darby.

Cam wasn't the only male seeking romance on this late spring evening. Peeper songs filled the night air, jangling like displaced sleigh bells, advertising their availability to any female within earshot. An occasional bullfrog chimed in with a bass note.

Luckier than the frogs, Cam had found his mate. Darby sprawled on a chaise lounge next to his Adirondack chair, occasionally sipping her beer, her pale face lifted to the stars as if counting them.

"Where do you see yourself in ten years?" He'd never asked a woman about the future before. Usually, he let his partner do all the talking. Although his past relationships had been exclusive, he hadn't invested in them. His last girlfriend left him because he couldn't always be available when she wanted him to be. He'd said, *you're right* and hadn't bothered to watch her leave.

Darby was different. Her response mattered.

"I'm not sure anymore. I always figured I'd get married, have a couple kids, keep working at the Local or someplace similar."

He liked the sound of that.

She sighed. "Astin upended my life with his bequest. So. In ten years. Hmm. I will have his Great Camp turned into a writing re-treat. An exclusive place for authors to come for uninterrupted soli-tude. Serve gourmet meals. Hospitality and culinary students at Paul Smith's College will compete for internships at the retreat. I'll offer college credit instead of a paycheck."

His alma mater. If he hadn't been in love with her before, he was now.

Slow down.

He'd already rushed her into a physical relationship. Not that she'd needed much persuasion. Except making love was a long way from getting married. He wanted forever from her. If he told her what he was thinking, she'd race to the county courthouse for an order of protection instead of a marriage license.

He dipped a toe into the water anyway. "Why don't you stay here for a while?"

"I can for a couple of nights." She shifted to face him. "Until my landlord replaces my locks. Not that I'll be living in the apartment much longer."

"Why not?" He sipped from his beer, gripping the dewy bottle more tightly than he needed to. It was too soon to hope she meant moving in with him.

"I'm moving to Nippletop."

"Nippletop?" She couldn't be serious.

"The Great Camp I inherited. You remember. The place we met. Rogue deer ticks? Mutating mosquitoes? Marijuana growers? I need to be on-premise to manage the retreat."

His gut clenched. "I knew what you meant. I don't think living there is a good idea."

"No choice. I'm the owner. I have to be on site. Continuing to pay rent on an apartment when I own property that's perfectly habitable doesn't make sense, so I'm moving. The timing works because my lease expires next month. I plan to pack my stuff between now and then and move a few boxes every day."

It was a miracle his beer bottle didn't shatter in his hand. He had no right to tell her what she could and couldn't do. He was her lover, not her keeper. Even after they were married, he could only express his opinions. His concerns. His fears.

"I'm not especially thrilled," she admitted. "I'm hoping I won't feel isolated once I book guests."

Would he be out of line if he suggested doing a background check on every visitor?

"I may convert the third-floor servant quarters in the lodge into an apartment. Or live in one of the cabins, but I'd rather keep those for guests. That's all for later, though. Until then, I'll be moving into Astin's former bedroom." She hesitated before asking, "What do you think?"

"I'd rather you were in my bedroom." He spoke bluntly. "The idea of you being there alone scares me, especially with Red Beard sniffing around. You'd be safer here."

"Maybe you could stay with me sometimes." The peepers nearly drowned out her words.

Sometimes? He wanted more than *some time* from her.

"I wouldn't mind seeing you again." She sounded unsure of herself. "I enjoyed being with you. Dinner. And after."

A loon yodeled in the distance.

"You mean making love?" He wanted to be very clear about what had transpired. "Because that's what I was doing, you know. Making love to you."

Her mouth opened and closed several times before she replied. "This is the twenty-first century. Just because we had sex, and it was my first time—"

He wouldn't let her diminish what he'd felt. Still felt. "I visited your camp this afternoon to ask you to dinner. I planned the invitation before you kissed me. Which I loved. I only wish the kiss had been real, not because you were frightened."

"Red Beard was an *excuse*," she repeated what she'd told him earlier. "I didn't even have to *think* about throwing myself at you. I seriously wanted to jump you the first time I saw you."

"Same." He cleared his throat as he placed his beer on the low table between them. "I fantasized about how I would love to be greeted by you like that every night after work."

He'd spent his whole life searching for this woman. He couldn't let his impatience drive her away.

People—okay, mostly men—had played heartless jokes on Darby. Big boobs and a matching booty made her a hard-to-miss target for malicious comments. Her April first birthday also made her a natural focus for hoaxes. The nastiness had gotten worse since Astin's ridiculous will became public. Cam? He seemed sincere.

Please don't let this be a prank.

He'd used the l-word.

What if he didn't mean what he'd said?

Be cool. She could do this. She'd been deflecting cruelty with humor her entire life.

Cam left his chair to sit on the floor next to her. He removed her beer from her hand and placed the bottle beside his on the table. His fingers were chilly and damp as they twined with hers. "I don't want you freaking out, thinking I'm a stalker or a controlling, manipulative guy. Okay?"

The crickets fell silent, as if they were eavesdropping.

"Okay." She did a gut-check. No warning tingles. Only the comfort and safety of his hand clasping hers. She'd learned to trust her instincts at an early age. Right now, they were curled up like her mother's cat, in a patch of sunshine, purring in his sleep.

He squeezed her fingers. "Do you believe in love at first sight?"

The peepers' song faded. The sky jettisoned stars to jitterbug in front of her eyes... or she was going to pass out from holding her breath, waiting for the punchline.

"I saw you standing on the porch at your camp, and I—oh, hell. I'm not good with words." His too-intense gaze left her face and focused elsewhere. "I just knew. Okay? It sounds crazy, but I knew we belong together."

"Wow." Other words failed her.

"I don't mean to rush you." He pulled her off the chaise and into his lap. The rasp in his voice agreed with his words. "The last thing I want to do is spook you. I'm nervous enough for us both."

He brushed a wayward curl off her cheek, then tilted her chin so he could cover her mouth with his.

Darby melted. Years of being considered an unattractive joke hadn't made her desperate for romance. Instead, her senses were sharper than they'd ever been.

No internal alarms clamored. The way Cam's mouth fit against hers, the caress of his tongue, his very taste awoke deep yearnings in her. And joy. She sensed no darkness in him.

If Cam Winehouse was going to upend her life, it would be for the better.

"We both have the next two days off. Right?" she asked when they paused to breathe.

"Yes." He nuzzled her neck, the stubble on his chin scraping her skin.

She tilted her head to give him better access. "We could spend them together. See what's what."

Explore the l-word.

She had to make sure sex wasn't making her stupid.

Cam's thumb brushed her hardening nipple, the heat of his hand seeping through the fleece of her shirt. "All you're giving me is two days?"

"For now."

Cam's conflicting thoughts battled for supremacy. Darby hadn't rejected him outright, even though he'd bungled it. She hadn't laughed when he asked about love at first sight. That was the most important thing.

"I need to think about it." She rested her head on his shoulder. "I don't make rash decisions. I wasted a month before accepting Astin's bequest. A relationship, especially with emotional commitment, is a lot bigger, a lot more important than inheriting property."

"That's fair." Cam admitted. Reluctantly. He decided not to mention purchasing an economy-sized box of condoms for a first date smacked of spontaneity. Everything about this day combined intuition and impulse. Unless she didn't consider physical intimacy important, and he wouldn't believe that for a second.

"And I still have to live at Camp Nippletop."

His job required him to live in his territory and work out of his home. Darby's property qualified. His wildest imaginings had never conjured a scenario where he'd be living in a historic Great Camp.

He hated the idea.

He chose his words carefully. "I'm worried about your safety there."

"Me, too," she admitted. "Especially after this afternoon. I need to buy defense spray. Maybe Dad will lend me his 12-gauge."

"Have you ever fired a shotgun?" He hated the weapon suggestion as much as he hated her being alone at the camp.

"Yes," she replied.

The park offered opportunities for seclusion. The same isolation invited criminal activity. Privacy—the main selling point Darby planned to offer authors—terrified Cam when it came to her well-being.

His job hours could be erratic. Any woman he married would be alone. A lot. Search and rescue operations occasionally required him to be on a mountain all night. He wanted Darby to be within calling distance of help, not isolated in the wilderness. Several law enforcement agencies populated Ray Brook—the federal prison, State Police Troop B headquarters, and the district office of the DEC.

Nippletop was a mountain. A lake. A Great Camp. All three were located several miles from another outpost of civilization.

Darby interrupted his musings with a yawn. "I'm sorry," she murmured, as she squirmed to her feet. "It's been a long day. And tomorrow promises to be another busy one."

Cam's lap felt empty without her weight pressing against him. He knew of one way to remedy the lack. He stood and offered his hand to her. "Bedtime?"

She didn't hesitate to grip his fingers.

He led her inside. For the first time in his life, he would sleep with the woman he loved in his arms. Maybe he was moving too fast for Darby's comfort, but he'd been waiting his whole life to meet her. To love her. If he could lock her up until Red Beard's arrest, he would. He couldn't risk her, and he didn't know how to make her understand without scaring her off.

CHAPTER SEVEN

TUESDAY, JUNE 13, 2000

Facing Cam in the morning wasn't as awkward as Darby had feared.

They were both early risers, despite not having slept much after they'd gone to bed. Cam apparently was working toward setting a record for most erections in a twenty-four-hour period. Muscles she'd never acknowledged introduced themselves to her in grumbling misery.

"We should have packed the food you bought for this morning," Cam said as he switched on the coffee. "I usually grab breakfast out. What time does your diner open?"

"Six."

Darby had pulled on her sweatsuit as soon as she crawled out of bed. She wasn't comfortable running around without clothes. Early mornings in the mountains were cool, even in high summer, a primary reason the wealthy had built their so-called "camps" in the Adirondacks. Even Cam, who gave off heat like a Saratoga County hot spring, wore sweatpants and a t-shirt.

Cam lured Darby to the deck with a mug of freshly brewed coffee. Gauzy mist draped the pond's surface. Birds cooed. A turtle plopped into the water.

Coffee *al fresco* meant more getting-to-know-you dialogue. Darby focused on favorites: colors, music, food, TV, movies. She figured they could get into astrological signs, religion, and politics later. Oh, and superheroes. Very important. After all, she couldn't marry a man who preferred Peter Parker to Clark Kent.

"I should hit the shower. I have a lot on my plate today, starting with calling my landlord about the locks and rescheduling with the contractor." Darby's jaw cracked as she yawned. She'd rather sit on Cam's deck and bask in the morning sun. She had promised him the time. "More coffee," she muttered.

She went inside and returned with the carafe.

"What happens if you don't make the camp into a hotel?" Cam extended his mug for a refill.

Darby poured as she considered her answer. "Writing retreat, not hotel. I have a year to get the retreat together. All I need is one paying author guest. Otherwise, the land reverts to the state. More public property for the forest preserve. The state will do its constitutionally mandated forever-wild thing and demolish the buildings."

"Would losing the camp be so bad?"

She set the carafe on the table. "Asks the man who works for the DEC."

He held up his hands. "To protect and preserve the natural resources of New York. That's my job."

Darby shrugged. "It doesn't matter. I am not going to fail. I have to change the name, though. Nippletop is too suggestive. Too bad Gothics Mountain isn't closer."

At his blank look, she explained: "Gothic is a type of mystery slash romance book. Nippletop sounds kinky."

His gaze rested on her breasts. One corner of his mouth lifted. "I'm fond of yours, and I'm willing to get kinky."

She didn't doubt him at all. She couldn't wear a bra beneath her sweatshirt this morning because the fabric chafed her nipples too much, yet her body reacted to his statements. Although she was positive Cam could see the effect his words had on her, she thrust out her chest to make sure.

He choked on his coffee. "You are an evil woman."

"Really?" She used the sweetest tone she could as she lifted the hem of her shirt and flashed him.

Cam's eyes nearly glowed. "Do you need help?"

Darby didn't know what had gotten into her. Besides Cam's penis. Maybe sex summoned her inner wild woman. "Nah." She yanked her sweatshirt into place. "I can manage. I'm an independent woman."

"Diabolical is more like it. Remember, though, payback's a bitch."

"I can't wait." She lifted her mug and sipped. His revenge didn't worry her. Retaliation gave her something else to anticipate.

In the meantime, she needed to focus on her agenda, primarily fulfilling the terms of Astin's will. Maybe Cam could help. "Can I bounce a few ideas off you?"

"Sure. I like most of your ideas." Innocuous words, but lecherous tone.

Her cheeks heated and her girl parts winced. Her mind jumped to places it shouldn't. Like imagining everything she wanted to do to him. With him. For him.

"I'm talking about the writing retreat," she mumbled, as much to keep herself on task as to chide him for tempting her. "Not payback."

"Damn. And here I thought we'd spend two days really getting to know each other."

"That's what I'm trying to do."

His grin faded. "You'd rather spend the day at your Great Camp. You're going to try to reschedule with the contractor for today."

Busted. "Not rather. But I only have eleven months to get everything ready for my first guests. And there's a lot to do."

Nippletop was her future. As crazy about Cam as she was, his status in her life was temporary. He could be gone by the day after tomorrow.

A muscle in Cam's cheek twitched. "Then I guess we'll be spending the day at the camp."

"I don't expect you to waste your day off—"

"I won't be wasting anything. I'm spending my day with you." He took her hands in his. Big, strong, capable hands. Memories of what his fingers had done to her in the past several hours flooded every crevice of her body. She could trust her life in those hands.

"Even if we hadn't already agreed to spend the next couple of days getting to know each other, I couldn't bear it if anything should happen to you," he murmured. "Concern is always going to shape my response to what you do. And you being alone out there worries me."

Would she ever get used to the intensity of his rusty gaze when it landed on her?

"Worry works two ways," she replied, struggling to keep her voice steady. The High Peaks were not a tame environment. She knew forest rangers took risks. "Your job is a lot more dangerous."

"Ranger qualification is a rigorous process," he reasoned. "I've had intensive and ongoing training in search and rescue, law enforcement, and firefighting. I have a team to back me up."

She couldn't argue with facts.

Cam was secure in his sense of self, while she resembled dandelion fluff. Well, not dandelion. Dandelion seeds were too delicate. Fragile. Maybe milkweed, a more substantial plant, but still adrift, looking for a place to grow and flourish.

Camp Nippletop—no, the James Coolidge Astin Memorial Writing Retreat—would give her a purpose. An identity of her own.

By the time Darby and Cam arrived at Chuck's Local Diner for breakfast, few open seats remained.

"Hi, Sue," Darby greeted her co-worker. "Mind if we take the corner booth?"

Darby spotted Sue's daughter sitting at the counter, her copper-colored curls absorbing all the light in the diner. "Sally can sit with us," Darby offered. "We'll buy her breakfast."

"Great." Sue smiled her relief. "She spent a week with her father at his church camp up near Cadyville. He just dropped her off. I've told him not to leave her here, but..."

Sally rolled her eyes. "*Atman* is not a church camp. It's an ashram. A spiritual retreat."

"Darby is opening a retreat, too," Cam interjected. "You can tell us about your dad's place."

Darby beamed at him. He'd known without her saying a word that Sally took up valuable real estate. By having her in the booth with them, another paying customer could sit at the counter. Then Chuck wouldn't give Sue a difficult time for having her kid hanging around, "using my diner for a damn day care center."

"Order whatever you want," Darby instructed Sally once they settled with their menus.

"Mom said she would get me something."

"Our treat." Darby knew Sue lived on a tight budget, so "something" could mean toast and water.

Sally's bright turquoise eyes clouded over, as if she were meditating. Then she nodded. "Okay. We'll barter."

After Sue took their orders, Darby pulled her notebook from her purse. "Here's my deal," she said to Sally, carrying out the pretense that she needed the girl's input. "I inherited a Great Camp to create a writing retreat. I know it's different from an ashram, but the general idea is the same. Getting away from the world to focus. I'm going to name it the James Coolidge Astin Memorial Writing Retreat."

"Too long," Cam said.

Darby ignored him. "I want four suites in the main lodge and three separate guest cabins. Seven total. I don't want to use numbers for designation. I'd prefer something more creative."

"Name them after the seven dwarves," Cam suggested. "Grumpy, Sneezy, Sleezy."

"Don't be silly," said the twelve-year-old. She pulled out a handful of colored rocks from her pocket. "And your boyfriend is right. The name is too long."

"Ranger Winehouse," Darby corrected the girl.

"He's your boyfriend. You're going to get married, have two sons, and live at the Great Camp." Sally stirred her stones with her index finger.

Darby and Cam stared at her.

"What?" Sally asked.

"That must be some ashram your dad has," Cam muttered.

"Nothing." Darby scowled at Cam. "Okay, what else comes in sevens? Days of the week? Seven seas? Seven continents?"

Cam negated Darby's suggestions. "Yeah, I'd pay to visit Antarctica, but I doubt most people would. And Monday? People hate Mondays."

"I think there are more than seven seas," Sally added.

"The seven deadly sins could be fun." Cam waggled his eyebrows at Darby.

Darby could remember only two, and headed off any discussion of lust in front of Sally by pointing out sloth would not be conducive to writing.

"The Write Place." Sally rearranged her stones.

Darby found the girl's actions spooky.

"You're creating a place for writers to write," Sally continued. "Call it what it is."

Darby had not expected Sally to contribute anything worthwhile, so a minute passed before she understood the child's meaning. "Oh. W-R-I-T-E place. That's good."

Cam sat back and stared at Sally. "Real good."

"And your rooms and cabins?" Sally spoke almost as if in a trance. "That's easy. Name them for the chakras."

"The what?" Darby asked.

Sally pushed a red stone to the middle of the table. "Chakras. There are seven of them. They're spiritual energy wheels in our bodies and align with the spine. The first one is the root or foundation chakra. It's red and means survival, security, safety."

When neither Darby nor Cam reacted, Sally nudged an orange stone below the red one. "Next would be sacral. Orange. For creativity."

Sally's expression turned sly. "Or sex."

Cam choked on his coffee.

One-by-one Sally positioned her stones as she explained. "Yellow. Solar plexus. Power and energy. Green. The heart. Love. Turquoise or blue. Throat. Communication and truth. Indigo. The brow or third eye. Wisdom and intuition. Violet. Crown. Spiritual connection."

"I could decorate each space with a color theme," Darby mused aloud. She opened her notebook and made a note.

"Yup," Sally agreed.

"Sounds like a rainbow to me," Cam muttered.

Sue arrived with their meals. "Will you put those rocks away," she scolded Sally, as she served the girl her eggs and toast. "You know I don't like that woo-woo stuff your father keeps brainwashing you with."

"They're not rocks, they're crystals." Sally scooped them from the table and returned them to her pocket.

"Don't pay any attention to her," Sue warned Cam and Darby, as she slid plates of french toast, home fries, and sausages onto the table. "Sally always comes back from her dad's acting weird."

"It's okay." Darby closed her book and reached for the saltshaker. "She solved a couple of dilemmas. I may have to hire her when she's old enough for her working papers."

"Really?" Sally's eyes widened. "Do you mean it?"

"Sure," Darby said. The kid would never remember. "You can be head of woo-woo."

"I'll study and practice really hard, so you won't regret it," Sally vowed.

"It's a deal. You'll have to explain the chakras again after we're done eating so I can write it down."

Cam rarely wore his service weapon while not on duty. Since he planned to stick to Darby like a burdock burr, he carried the Sig Sauer. Especially since she insisted on meeting the contractor at the camp.

"We should paint our bedroom orange," he said, as he drove them toward Nippletop. "You know. The sex chakra to keep us in the mood."

Darby swatted his arm. "I doubt you need any outside help. Like naming the rooms after the deadly sins. You were going to suggest lust, weren't you. I kept waiting for you to insist Horny is one of the seven dwarves."

He leered. "Now that you mention it—is Astin's bed still in the lodge?"

He'd never wanted to be inside a woman as much as he did Darby. "Maybe we can grab a quickie."

"Seriously?" Her voice squeaked. "Don't you need time to recuperate?"

"What can I say?" He squeezed her thigh. "You motivate me."

"Pay attention to the road, Ranger Winehouse. How much did you pay Sally to predict our marriage?"

"I didn't." Chills had marched along Cam's spine when the kid spoke. "I've never seen her before in my life. Is she a psychic? Does she always pop out with weird stuff?"

"According to her mother. Sometimes Sue worries her ex is giving her drugs. She had Sally tested once, but nothing showed up."

"She nailed everything. The Write Place. Naming the rooms and cabins." He glanced at Darby. "Us getting married."

"Two sons? I'm going to be outnumbered in my own house. New rule. Toilet seats down."

Cam laughed. Darby had admitted they were going to get married and have kids. Two boys he could teach to fish, to appreciate the wilderness. He couldn't wait.

He pulled onto the dirt lane leading to the Great Camp. The parking area was empty. The pressure in his chest eased. He parked in front of the porch.

Darby climbed out and mounted the steps. She stood facing the woods, her eyes closed, and inhaling deeply.

Cam didn't need an explanation. He often performed a similar ritual, letting the pure Adirondack air and nature's symphony center him. Absorbing the atmosphere made him a better man. Hell, he could follow suit right now. If he had to live here, he needed to imprint Camp Nippletop on his psyche.

Not Nippletop. The Write Place. He had to make the camp his right place. The right and safe place for his family.

When he opened his eyes, he found Darby studying him.

"Did you hear any rogue deer ticks? Smell any defecating moose?"

He joined her on the porch. "Nope. All seems to be well."

She snagged his hand. "Let's go in. I'll give you the fifty-cent tour while we wait for the contractor."

Cam had never been inside a Great Camp structure. Leftovers from the Gilded Age, the elaborate compounds were the footprints of the wealthy who'd once flocked to mountains to escape city life. Fire had claimed many buildings. Others were demolished or neglected into decay. The National Historic Register listed several.

Nippletop occupied none of those categories.

Cam's first impression of the main room was that it could use a good cleaning. There was nothing special about the space except an enormous fireplace. A bear pack could use the firebox as a cave to hibernate for the winter. Cobwebs draped the antlers of the mandatory moose head mounted above the mantel. Faded ethnic-style rugs strewn across the beat-up wood floors needed more than vacuuming.

"This will be the lobby. The reception area. A place for socializing if the guests want to mingle." Darby stood by the fireplace and gestured at various areas. "A couple of cushy sofas here. Maybe a breakfast buffet on the weekends."

"Don't forget a table for Sally's crystal ball."

Darby choked. "Very funny. She won't remember what happened today. And if she does, I'll put her in the game room with a Ouija board."

Cam knew better. "Game room?"

"In Astin's office." She opened a door to reveal an even darker, dingier area. A massive desk with a typewriter off to one side dominated the room. Bookcases lined the walls. A plethora of items—including a human skull—filled the shelves. Piles of old newspapers and magazines behind the desk created both a haven for rodents and a fire hazard.

"Picture card tables, comfortable reading chairs, board games, maybe a library... someday."

"You're going to need a dumpster," Cam muttered.

"On my list. I also need to get an appraiser in here." She sighed. "At least Chatham has a comprehensive inventory. He's been worried about someone looting the place."

Cam clenched his teeth. He couldn't picture himself living here, much less raising a family in such bleak surroundings.

Camp Nippletop's only redeeming quality was the lake. The views from the wall of windows at the rear of the lodge were stunning. He squinted at the lopsided dock and tried to conjure images of his alleged future sons sitting there, fishing poles in hand.

Nothing.

On the other hand, he could buy a canoe or kayak, neither of which his pond in Ray Brook could accommodate.

A man's voice calling, "Anybody here?" interrupted Cam's ruminations.

Cam grabbed Darby's arm to keep her from dashing outside. "Let me go first," he practically growled at her. He unsnapped his holster, readying his gun.

Darby stepped aside.

"Can I help you?" Cam asked the husky blond man who stood on the front porch. A black pickup with a magnetic sign stating the vehicle belonged to Two Olympic Builders sat next to Cam's SUV. Yes, Cam had seen the trucks around. Signs meant nothing.

"Yeah, I'm supposed to meet a Darby Remington about an estimate. That you?"

"That's me." Darby pushed her way past Cam. "Sorry about the mix-up yesterday."

"Gotta admit I considered not rescheduling with you. I'm Joe, by the way. The guy who met me here yesterday—"

"A trespasser," Cam said.

Joe's attention slid to Cam's holster. "A boss can't be too careful who he works for or where he sends his crews. I didn't like that guy."

"Neither do we," Cam said. "The gun is a precautionary measure after yesterday."

"Like I said on the phone, I don't want my guys working here if he's around."

"He won't be a problem." Darby spoke firmly. "Let's get started. I'm sure you're a busy man."

"I am. You should have called a couple of months ago if you want anything done this year. Summer is our busy season."

"I didn't inherit Nippletop until a couple months ago. Besides, most of what I need done is interior work. Rainy day stuff, right? Let's start at the top and work our way down."

Darby led the men up the steep stairs to the top floor.

Spending the night at Cam's had given her ideas about what she wanted for her —their—living quarters. Even if they didn't get married, Cam's place featured amenities she envied. Meanwhile, she would pretend everything Sally Stone said was true.

That meant Cam's needs had to figure into her plans. He loved the outdoors and revered nature. Sure, the state paid him to patrol the Adirondack Park's forests and mountains, but he also found solace in nature. His home should be a sanctuary. They could rehab one of the Great Camp's outbuildings into a work base for him.

Whether or not she and Cam ended up together, Darby would live on site. The Great Camp meant more than a career and business for her. Hopefully, she'd be raising a family here. Until Cam invited her to stay with him, she hadn't considered what her home should be. Until last night's break-in at her apartment, she hadn't thought about home being a safe place. Until Cam, she hadn't thought about a home of her own at all. Not even at Nippletop.

The third-floor rooms were small, dark, and cramped. They would be unbearably hot come July. "I'd like this area to be an apartment for a family," she announced. "Skylights. I want a balcony overlooking the lake. An eat-in kitchen. A primary bedroom with its own bathroom. Can you tap into the chimney for a woodstove in the living room? Oh, and I need a dumbwaiter. For hauling stuff up and down the stairs. A laundry chute, too."

She glanced at Cam. "Do you have any suggestions or ideas?"

He'd crossed his arms. "No."

The single word combined with his body language conveyed more about his opinion than a library filled with dictionaries and thesauruses could.

"Do you have the architectural drawings for changes to the structure?" Joe asked.

Darby stared at him. "I'm sorry?"

"Essex County building codes require an architect's stamp on the blueprints for any major structural changes," Joe explained. "You could run into other issues if the camp is on the National Register of Historic Places."

"It's not on the register. I didn't realize I'd need an architect." Disappointment formed a lump in her throat. One more roadblock. Her only hope for booking a paying guest within the next eleven months rested in the outbuildings. "Can you look at the cabins? I don't think they need major restructuring."

Chapter Eight

"I don't think living on the third floor is a good idea," Cam said, as he and Darby stood on the porch and watched Joe's truck depart. Seeing the space had confirmed his worst fears.

"What? Yeah, it's currently not habitable, but—"

"Let's start with the third floor is a firetrap. There's only one staircase in and out."

"I'm sure the building code will require a fire escape."

"I don't care." Cam refused to budge. If he had to live here because his woman lived here, he damn well would have his say. "This is a wooden building that's over a hundred years old. Do you have any idea how quickly it would burn?"

Darby said nothing.

"I would have nightmares about you and the boys being trapped. How could you carry two kids down a fire escape if I was on wilderness foot patrol?" He purposely invoked Sally's prediction to strengthen his argument.

"You have a point," Darby conceded. She sank to the top step of the porch and pulled her knees to her chest, wrapping her arms around them as if she needed an anchor.

He sat next to her, close enough for their hips to brush, his legs stretched toward the ground. "Forget fire. Let's say an intruder came after you. You'd be trapped on the third floor. You'd have no way to escape. We can convert an outbuilding into a house for us."

If he kept talking about their life together and the children Sally claimed they'd have, maybe Darby would commit to a shared future.

"I get why you believe you have to live here, even if I don't agree or particularly like the idea," he continued. "But please, reconsider living on the third floor."

"Fine. We compromise. Right?"

The tightness in his chest eased. She heard him, understood his concerns.

"Instead of converting outbuildings into staff housing, I can put them on the third floor and let them die if the place catches fire."

"They won't have children to carry down a fire escape." He could be reasonable. "Let's forget fire and talk about hauling the boys up and down the stairs any time they wanted to play outside. Or did you plan to use the dumbwaiter for them?"

Darby rested her chin on her upraised knees. "You're making too many good points. Besides, the boys will need a yard to play in."

"Fenced-in yard," Cam corrected. Mentally, he pumped his fist. She, too, spoke as if their sons were real. "The lake is too close."

"You think of everything."

He couldn't decide if she complimented or chided him. "I'm trained to search for problems and prevent accidents."

"Are you limited to the physical? Like hikers who don't carry enough water or flashlights?"

He narrowed his eyes. "Where are you going with this?"

She drew her knees closer to her chest. "Maybe you're better off not knowing."

Darby should have kept her mouth shut. But no, she had to dangle her concerns like a fly dive-bombing a frog. So childish, as if she were playing a game with Cam. Except she didn't know how else to approach the topic without opening a carton of fat, slimy night-crawlers.

On the other hand, Cam fished. He'd know what to do with a disgusting glob of worms.

His face revealed nothing as he waited for her to elaborate.

"After Red Beard showed up and claimed he'd done business with Astin, I got to wondering what Astin did with the money Red Beard allegedly paid him. What if he mixed drug money in with the trust fund?" The question had weighed on her since Red Beard. "Would the government be able to seize my assets? Take the land?"

"Not the land. You only recently inherited it. As soon as you suspected illegal activity, you brought in law enforcement. I reported finding what appears to be preparations for a marijuana field. The break-in and threat at your apartment—which you also reported—came after my observation. You're cooperating with officials."

Cam sounded as if he'd researched the possibility.

No, her conscience reminded her, *he's in law enforcement. He knows the laws regarding illegal growing in the Adirondacks.*

"Where did the money in the trust fund come from?" Cam asked.

"I assume from royalties. He published a lot of books. Won literary prizes. Someone wanted to make a movie out of one of his novels—they optioned the rights. Nothing ever came of it, and Astin got to keep the money."

"You're kidding."

"No one around here knew. Except, apparently, me." She sighed and slumped, feeling like a deflated balloon. "Without the trust fund, I can't make this place into a retreat. I can't hire an architect to rehab the second and third floors, much less have the contractor reconfigure the outbuildings."

Cam rubbed her nape. "You're borrowing trouble."

"No, I'm protecting my business." She needed to be prepared for the worst-case scenario. Even grouchy Chuck planned for emergencies at the diner.

So did Cam when he hiked his territory. She'd seen the enormous, dark green backpack hanging near his door, stocked and ready to go.

"Tell me, what's in your work backpack? The one you wear while you're patrolling."

"Snacks. Water. Medical gear. Matches. A couple of headlamps. A space blanket. Stuff I might need if I'm doing search and rescue." He hesitated to share the information.

"You just proved my point."

He narrowed his eyes. "They're not the same."

"Are too. You make contingency plans based on possibilities. What kind of businesswoman would I be if I didn't do the same?"

"I hate when you're right," he admitted after a moment. "Have you mentioned your concerns to the attorney? You can call him when we get back to my place."

"Why don't I call him now?" Darby climbed to her feet.

Cam pulled out his cell phone and checked the bars. "No service."

Darby chuckled and extended her hand to him. "On the landline, silly."

Cam's stunned expression was priceless. "You have a landline?"

"Yes."

He grabbed her hand and yanked her onto his lap. "All this time you let me worry you didn't have a way to call for help?"

"No *cell* phone service. I never mentioned a landline. You found my home number with no problem. I assumed you could get Astin's unlisted number."

"You are truly diabolical," he said, before silencing any response she might have made by kissing her.

His scent overwhelmed her. She'd never noticed how a man smelled, unless he needed a shower, yet Cam's aroma wended into all her secret places. His mouth on hers, his tongue tantalizing hers, only intensified the combined traces of balsam, cedar, and moss, creating a cologne called "Cameron."

Forget about sex making her stupid. A simple kiss from him reduced her to gibberish and drool. Except his kisses weren't simple, and she couldn't afford to be distracted. She broke off the kiss.

"I have to call the attorney." The words sounded as if she'd gasped them. She placed her forefinger against his lips. "Remember where we were."

She extracted herself and fled on shaky legs to Astin's study.

Cam followed.

Astin had updated his phone in the 1980s. He'd programed his attorney, Howard Chatham, into the speed dial. She sat in the creaky leather chair to make the call.

When she got Chatham on the line, she said, "I'm going to put you on speakerphone so my..." she didn't know how to refer to Cam.

"Fiancé," Cam supplied.

"My forest ranger friend can hear our conversation."

Joking around about Sally Stone's blathering was one thing. Calling Cam her fiancé to an attorney was another.

Chatham agreed to be placed on speaker.

She voiced her concerns and asked her questions, then listened to Chatham parrot everything Cam had told her. He added, "I can assure you all the money in the trust comes from Astin's writing. Have you considered the possibility your trespasser lied to you?"

"No. Someone broke into my apartment last night."

"Someone left a threat in her apartment last night," Cam clarified, then launched into his account of yesterday afternoon.

He sounded weary of having to repeat his story. She regretted drawing him into her mess. Except he'd suggested he poke around after encountering Red Beard. Cam's decision. Cam's responsibility as a ranger.

Chatham confirmed Cam's theory that because she'd immediately alerted the authorities—in other words, Cam—she was in the clear.

She ended the conversation, then opened her notebook to the current version of her never-ending to-do list.

Cam leaned against the door frame of Darby's bedroom, watching her stuff clothes into a duffel and feeling as useless as bullets without a gun. He'd felt the same way most of the day.

At least she packed more than a night or two worth of underwear, jeans and shirts.

"Want me to order a pizza?" If he didn't find something to occupy himself, he'd implode. "We can pick it up on the way to my place."

"Sure. Or we can have it delivered here. The number is on my speed dial."

"I'd rather eat on my deck." He'd spent the day in her space, from breakfast at the Local, to meeting the contractor at the camp and the aftermath, and now in her apartment. He needed to breathe his own air while he still possessed some.

"Should we check our pizza add-on compatibility?" she asked, as she rifled through a drawer.

Cam snickered. "'What's your topping' is probably a more reliable gage than 'what's your sign'."

"What *is* your sign?"

"I have no idea," he lied. He considered horoscopes on the same level as palm reading and seances. Woo-woo didn't interest him—except when Sally Stone predicted his and Darby's marriage and family.

"When's your birthday?" Darby pressed.

He didn't want to answer. His February fourteenth birthday embarrassed him, as much as an adult as in childhood. Women tried to make any celebration deeper than he wanted. He refused to get sentimental about a greeting-card holiday. Then again, he'd never been in love. Until now.

"No date can be any worse than mine," she stated when he didn't answer. "I hate my birthday. I am permanently traumatized by the practical jokes played on me as a child."

"You're an April Fools baby?" He laughed.

She threw a balled-up pair of socks at him.

"I hate my birthday, too," he confessed. "February fourteenth."

"Your birthday is Valentine's Day? People must go broke buying cards for you."

He didn't want to discuss the hearts and lace and all the shades of red he'd endured his entire life. "What do you want on your pizza?"

"Anchovies and pineapple."

He snorted. "I don't think so. Mushrooms."

She tilted her head, as if considering his suggestion. "Extra cheese?"

"If you insist."

"I do."

"Then I insist we use my favorite pizzeria and eat at my house." Did he know how to negotiate or what?

"Fine." She sighed as she peered around the dimly lit room. "I'd hoped changing the locks would make me more comfortable after last night's break-in. Nope. I doubt I'll ever be able to sleep here again."

"Luckily, you don't have to." Cam had examined the new locks. The landlord's installation didn't impress him. Good thing she'd be staying with him.

"Right." She returned to pawing through her clothes.

Cam could use a beer and a couple of slices. The day had been tension-filled in unfamiliar ways. Besides, he wanted to be in his house while he still could. No way would he allow Darby to live at Nippletop—er, the Write Place—on her own. At least the Great Camp's location fulfilled his job requirement to live within his territory.

"Why don't I pack up your fridge?" he offered. Ordering a pizza didn't qualify as work. Everything else could wait until she moved to the Great Camp.

She dropped two duffels by the back door. "That's okay. I'll do it."

"What? You don't trust me to save your bacon or protect your eggs?"

"Funny. I don't want to put you out any more than I already have."

Cam resisted the urge to pat her ass as she brushed past him. Nor did he use her opening for another double-entendre remark. He would put out for her anytime she wanted.

She didn't comment on his restraint as she transferred food from the refrigerator into plastic grocery bags. Maybe she hadn't noticed. Maybe she wasn't as sexually attuned to him as he was to her. He refused to believe he was thinking with his dick, as women so often accused men of doing. He was thinking with his heart.

"Order the pizza. If you get one from your place, the crust better be a New York-style thin one, or you'll be eating anchovy and pineapple pizza until you die."

In the good news category, she spoke of forever with him. The bad news? She didn't trust him enough to order a pizza. "Why won't you let me do something?"

"I know where everything is. If you want to help, you can carry my bags to your SUV." She spoke without looking at him.

Okay. She'd given him a task. Something positive. His SUV occupied her spot behind the bakery. The parking lot provided another reason for her to move. Five o'clock on a mid-June afternoon, while daylight prevailed, the isolation didn't matter. Much. Except by late August, the shadows would deepen by six. He'd seen the piss-poor lighting the landlord provided.

In the end, Darby packed only two duffels and two bags of groceries. He called his favorite pizza shop while Darby fumbled with the new locks. She'd insisted she needed to learn their quirks, as if she planned on living in the apartment again.

More good news: they favored the same pizzeria. The corresponding bad news came when Darby insisted on paying for the pie. "You bought breakfast. And dinner last night."

"Dinner was a date," Cam reminded her through clenched teeth as they returned to his vehicle. The pizza box warmed his hands. "And you bought breakfast, too."

"We didn't eat the breakfast I bought."

"We will tomorrow. What is going on with you?" Cam put the pizza in back with her clothes and perishable food items.

Darby didn't respond until they were in his SUV.

"Too much togetherness too soon." She pulled her shoulder harness into place and latched it.

Something in his chest tightened. They hadn't even made it one day.

"Tuesdays and Wednesdays are my weekend. I usually do laundry, housework, visit my parents—domestic stuff. Now I have cleaning out the lodge and packing my apartment added to my chores. I feel guilty for not interacting with you more, especially when spending the day together was my idea. Now you've wasted your day off. But, on the other hand, I never asked you to guard me."

He put his vehicle in gear and pulled onto the street. Truthfully? He resented—a bit—that he'd spent his day off not tending to his own chores. He, too, had household puttering to do, but those tasks became inconsequential when compared to Darby's safety.

"Remind me again why I'm moving my clothes to your cabin."

"Someone broke into your place and plunged a steak knife through a stack of condoms, so you're staying with me until the perpetrator is caught." He would never forget the sight of the blade mutilating Darby's hopes for the evening.

"Right." She huffed out her breath. "I keep trying to forget because it scares me."

She was frightened. Good. She should be.

The pressure in his chest eased. The intensity of his feelings for her terrified him, so he could relate.

"You enjoy making love with me," he added in a soft voice.

"How could I forget the sex? I can barely sit, much less walk."

"I didn't say sex." Guilt jabbed at him. He knew he should have been more careful with her, especially after discovering her inexperience. "I said making love."

"I know you did, but I'm trying to keep it in context. It's too soon to use the l-word."

"What word would you prefer?" He couldn't hide his annoyance. "Intercourse? Fornicate? Fucking?"

She flinched. "Don't be crude."

"That's my point." He tried to soften his tone. "Every time I look at you, breathe in your scent, touch you—I'm loving you."

He reached across the console and covered her hand. "You're starting a whole new life. I understand. And here I am, wanting even more from you."

Forever, if he had his way.

"I'm overwhelmed. Maybe because I didn't get much sleep last night." She twined her fingers in his. "I'm not an impulsive person. Usually. Except with you. And that's unsettling. What if what I'm feeling is only lust?"

He glanced at her again. The SUV swerved. He corrected the course immediately, jostling the pizza box and sending a burst of garlicky aroma into the air.

She admitted to feelings for him. Undefined at that moment, but even that fragment gave him hope.

"You distract me too much," she continued. "Now you're in my head, and I can't compartmentalize you out of my day-to-day. At least, not today. Or yesterday."

Maybe he lived in her head, but she'd crept into his soul, which might be the stupidest thing he'd ever believed. His obsession worried him. Excited him. Confused him.

"I know what you mean." He squinted as the road twisted and the sun hit his eyes.

"Do you?"

Another glance at her showed she was finally looking at him.

"Let's say we actually get married." She squeezed his fingers. "Scared yet?"

He wanted to laugh. "Not scary." *That's what I've wanted since we met.*

"Two kids, like Sally said."

"I'm with you so far. I'd like to wait a few years, but yeah. At least two. I can afford a family. How many, though, will be your decision. Your body will do all the work. And, being realistic, you'll be the primary parent. My job, well, as you'll find out, my hours can be erratic."

"Oh." She took her time processing what he'd said.

His attitude had to score points in his favor. His words weren't lip service. He'd seen how pregnancy wore out his sister. Children were needy. They required time he might not have to give them. Darby would have the final say in how many children.

She cleared her throat. "Living at my writing retreat."

His sticking point. The isolated Great Camp. Leaving Darby and their future children alone there while he did his job.

At least he'd convinced her to abandon her third-floor apartment idea.

"Nippletop—The Write Place—is nonnegotiable," she said, as if reading his mind. "Unless I fail. That's something you don't know about me. Once I decide something, I'm in for the long haul. I intend to succeed."

"What about us?"

"Come on. It's barely been twenty-four hours since you invited me to dinner."

"Since you kissed me," he reminded her.

"Since I threw myself at you," she corrected. "Lust."

"Lust isn't such a bad thing." He liked it just fine.

"But is sex enough for a marriage?" Darby released his hand and returned to the scenery. "I have a cousin who got incredibly stupid from sex. Her husband belittles her. Tries to control her every action. Knocks her around. And she lets him. I don't think she loves him, but she's dependent on him. I'm sure he cheats on her. Sex scrambled her brains."

"I have never hit a woman in my life." The idea sickened him. That Darby would think he would abuse her pissed him off. "I'm not him."

"If I thought you were, I wouldn't be here."

Cam gripped the steering wheel tighter. "And I don't cheat. What did I tell you last night?"

"You majored in Environmental Science at Paul Smith's. Hunting turns you off, but you love to fish. You think camping on a beach is a great time." She rattled off bits from their dinner conversation. Paused. "You don't do casual sex, so any relationship you have is exclusive."

She turned toward him. "This morning I learned your favorite color is blue, and if you must listen to music, you prefer country. Your favorite TV show is *Survivor*, and you're a meat-and-potatoes man. You're a Valentine's Day baby. Did I miss anything?"

"Yeah." He kept his eyes on the road. "I'm worried sick about you being alone at your camp."

He didn't mean to snarl the last word. He tried to continue in a more reasonable tone. "Every instinct I have tells me Red Beard isn't finished with you, and that terrifies me."

Cam hated admitting fear. He'd battled wildfires, captured armed felons on the lam, and rescued injured hikers during blizzard conditions while dangling from a state police helicopter. Nothing twisted his guts like the idea of an illegal grower going after the woman he wanted to marry.

"I'm scared, too," she quietly confessed. "Everything about Nippletop scares me. Oh, heck, you scare me."

Cold washed through him. "I scare you," he carefully repeated once he could speak again. He thought they'd settled sex-equals-abuse.

"Yeah. For once in my life, I had a plan." She sounded miserable. "Astin must have seen a potential in me. No one else ever has. He offered me a chance to succeed. An opportunity to do something besides refill coffee cups at the Local."

Cam thought he heard a sniffle.

"Now you're asking me to put my plan on hold, and I *like* you. Today. And I'm considering a future with you."

Thank God.

"And you want me to give up my chance for... validation. Sex makes women stupid."

Oh, hell. Shit, damn piss, and fuck. He'd screwed up. Now he needed to fix it.

Being a forest ranger provided him with a structure in which to live his values. He enjoyed the physicality of the work and the autonomy the profession allowed him. He'd chosen the job because he believed in its purpose. He understood Darby needed a similar vocation.

Why did her validation have to be at Camp Nippletop? Couldn't she write books or refinish furniture or quilt? Garden?

He swallowed hard and hoped he wasn't digging himself in deeper.

"I'm not asking you to give up your plans." He wanted her to, though. "I simply want you to be careful. I *need* to know you're safe. Yeah, yeah. Life offers no guarantees. Shit happens. Having illegal growers after you magnifies all the risks."

She said nothing.

"Don't break my heart," he whispered.

He'd put everything out there, and she had nothing to say. Talk about a fuck up.

"Darby—"

"I can't sit back and wait for something to happen." The words burst from her, but her voice warbled. "Astin gave me one year to transform the camp into a retreat, and I wasted a month debating whether to accept the challenge. I am not trying to give you a hard time, and I have no intention of breaking your heart. I hope you'll treat mine with the same respect."

"Hard to respect you if you're dead." Speaking through clenched teeth felt more controlled than if he shouted at her, which is what he wanted to do.

"And I don't want to die before I've had a chance to live," she retorted. "Life is tough. What about you? You could encounter illegal growers while you're doing your job. You could have run into Red Beard while you inspected my property yesterday. Don't you patrol a lot of remote terrain? Aren't those places more likely to attract growers than a Great Camp where people are coming and going? Let's not mention the other two-legged dangers—the meth cookers, paramilitary cults, and human traffickers. And bears. Let's not forget bears."

She inhaled deeply and spoke in a calmer voice. "What if I said I didn't want you doing search and rescue in the middle of the night when a hiker falls from a cliff? The mountains are perilous enough in daylight. At night? In the rain? Snow? Are you crazy? But I wouldn't ask you to stop. I respect what you do too much. I respect you too much."

He loved how she refused to take any grief from him and continued to stick up for what she wanted. If only asserting herself didn't put that same self in danger.

"Besides," she continued in a more reasonable tone, "we haven't confirmed Red Beard is a grower. Or that he was the one who broke into my apartment. Anyone could have."

"You felt threatened by Red Beard, and that's good enough for me," Cam stated.

Chapter Nine

D arby straightened in her seat. Something clicked inside her. Something important.

Cam Winehouse did not dismiss her reaction to Red Beard. He believed her. Trusted her instincts. Instead of a *there, there,* and a pat on the head, he validated her. She heard his belief as loudly and as clearly as if he'd spoken aloud.

"Thank you." She could barely get the words out. No one ever took her seriously. Cam constantly upset her world. His motivation wasn't to stop her from opening the writing retreat, but to protect her.

His concern made her feel treasured, a fragile and embarrassing reaction.

"I need time to figure stuff out. I'm usually not such a scatterbrain."

"Everything is coming at you at once. I get it."

But did he? Common female wisdom claimed men thought with their dicks instead of their brains. What if she was doing the same thing? She tried to unravel the sex from the rest of her emotions, figuring lust and her newly awakened libido were adding to her confusion.

A week ago, if anyone had told her she would be head-over-heels with a guy she'd just met, she'd accuse them of being drunk.

Two months ago, she'd have asked anyone who told her she'd inherit a Great Camp to transform into a destination for artsy-fartsy types if they were on crack.

She knew the latter to be true, so why couldn't the former also be a fact? Could she trust her instincts regarding him?

"I'm sorry I'm not listening to you." Cam surprised her when he broke the awkward silence. "Or rather, not absorbing what you're saying to me."

A weight in her chest dissolved.

"I'm rushing you," he admitted. "I've been waiting a long time to find you. Relationship stuff is all new to me, too. I want to move forward. Everybody has a deadline, and no one is considering what you want. You have eleven months to get Nippletop converted into The Write Place. Contractor problems alone are going to mess with your deadline. You don't need me pressuring you, too."

Everything in her life, including her expectations and her focus, had been skewed upside down, sideways, or smashed to smithereens.

A deer bounded out of the trees and crossed the road in front of them. If Darby didn't know it was anatomically impossible, she would have sworn her heart leaped into her throat.

The sudden motion didn't faze Cam. Oh, he swore, reduced his speed, and peered into the trees lining the road, as if searching for more movement, but he didn't lose control. He remained outwardly calm. He handled the unexpected better than she did. His self-assurance intimidated her. His attention thrilled her.

She wondered if she should be wary. Sexy hunks didn't fall for frumpy, overweight waitresses. Cam could be with her because she'd inherited Camp Nippletop. More people—and he could be one—were aware of her since Astin's bequest became public. The property was valuable, a rare privately owned parcel surrounded by state-owned forever-wild land.

Why would a forest ranger come to a Great Camp to warn the occupant about an escaped convict? Wouldn't the state police do the notifications?

Almost the first words Cam spoke had been about illegal growers.

No. No. The state police had confirmed Cam reported finding a possible pot field at Nippletop. That's why they'd been quick to respond when the Saranac Lake police called about her apartment being broken into. She was being paranoid and ridiculous. Troopers and rangers worked together all the time.

"Do you trust me?" Cam asked after several silent moments.

"If I didn't, I wouldn't be here."

"Or you have no other choice."

She studied his profile. "Not true. I could stay in my apartment. The landlord replaced the locks. My family would gladly put me up. I could even stay at Nippletop. You are not my last resort."

"I want to be your best option."

"I'm here," she repeated. "My clothes are with me. There are mushrooms on the pizza."

"Right. Mushrooms on the pizza."

"And 33 condoms in my duffel."

"I have my own condoms," he reminded her. "Unless you don't trust them."

"I want to make sure we don't run out. And before you get all insulted and hurt because I'm maligning your manhood, having extra condoms is not a reflection on your staying power or recuperation time. It's being prepared for the worst-case scenario. Like your backpack. And, so you're aware, I plan to call the clinic tomorrow to discuss birth control."

He didn't react.

Darby swallowed hard. He couldn't have said, *thank you?* Maybe he didn't understand what a huge step making that call was for her. She pushed forward. "We've never discussed contraception beyond using condoms, and as you're aware, I'm clean—"

"I'm clean, too. I can show you the results of my last physical."

He sounded as if he were speaking through gritted teeth.

"I believe you. That's why I'm calling the clinic."

Cam exhaled. Loudly. "Okay. Can you deal with contraception until we're ready to start our family? Then, after we have our two boys, I'll get a vasectomy."

How could this man turn her to mush? "That's a brilliant plan." *If we get married.*

"Way better than pineapple on a pizza," he agreed.

"Have you ever eaten pineapple on a pizza?" she asked.

"No."

"Then how do you know you won't like it? Sometimes you have to take risks."

Cam peered at his pond. He would miss sitting on his deck in the fading summer light and listening to the wildlife serenade him. Whenever he could, he ate his meals at the round table. He could put the table on the back porch at Darby's lodge, facing Nippletop Lake. But people would be around. Strangers. Employees. His job, educating the public about using state lands, could be frustrating. Those were the days he needed to come home to solitude.

At least Darby was including him while making plans for her property. She'd asked for his input. "You'll need an outbuilding for your work stuff," she'd declared. Her suggestion implied trust. Acknowledged a future together.

The woman had him tied in knots. She might claim sex made women stupid, but men weren't immune to being pussy whipped.

He bit into his pizza.

Darby sat across from him, lost in her own thoughts. Probably making another list, although he didn't see her notebook. A breeze ruffled the dark curls brushing her shoulders. This is how he wanted to spend the rest of his life, sitting with her, absorbing the quiet, anticipating getting her naked.

She glanced up and caught him staring. Her tentative smile radiated beauty. Everything about Darby amazed him. And he would blow their relationship if he didn't ease back on his overwhelming need to protect her.

Trust required a two-way street, and he needed to trust her to be cautious. He'd witnessed her awareness of her surroundings—she'd noticed Red Beard's license plate. She'd double-checked locking her door before going out at night. But for all her talk of pepper spray and 12-gauge shotguns, she remained unarmed. The gun idea bothered him, but he could help with the OC spray. The state allowed oleoresin capsicum spray in bigger containers for law enforcement. Giving his to her wasn't legal or ethical, and he could get into trouble if anyone ever found out, but he could deal with the consequences if he had to. He'd rather have her safe.

Darby wadded her used napkin and tossed it on to her grease-stained paper plate. "Pizza was a good idea. Thanks." She lifted her beer.

"Thanks for buying," he replied.

He piled their debris on the pizza box's closed top. He'd grab his OC spray while he was thinking about it. "Need anything from inside? Another beer?"

"I'm good." She stretched her legs.

Plates and napkins to the trash. Check. Leftover pizza in the refrigerator. Check. Remove the defense spray cannister from his duty belt. Nope. Seeing his handcuffs distracted him. He glanced at the door to the deck.

Too bad his new inspiration would waste daylight, but the mosquitos, black flies, and no-see-ums would consider naked human bodies a feast. Plus, not letting Darby swat at dining insects would be cruel and unusual punishment. Especially since he wanted her to trust him.

"Hey, Darby. Can you come in here?"

Darby opened her eyes. She didn't want to move. Sitting on Cam's deck with a beer as the day faded allowed the tension to seep from her bones. She envied his deck and hoped she could create something similar at Nipple—The Write Place, even if she couldn't have her third-floor balcony.

However, true love beckoned tonight.

True love? Hah! What did she know about man-woman love? Cam was as close to being her first boyfriend since second grade. She couldn't help but wonder if her feelings were more of a desperate latching on to male attention than true affection.

She had to stop obsessing about her relationship with Cam and take it day by day.

She pushed away from the table and stood. Her spine cracked.

It would take time for her to get used to the camp's name change, she thought as she ambled into Cam's house. Sally Stone was one scary child, but she'd nailed the perfect name for what James Coolidge Astin had envisioned.

What else had Sally gotten right?

And here she was, obsessing again.

She didn't see Cam in the kitchen. "Where are you?"

"Bedroom."

"Figures," she muttered. She hadn't exaggerated when she told him her girl bits were more than a little tender. Yet her nipples tingled, and heat pooled low in her belly. Cam would more than compensate for any discomfort.

She found him in the bedroom, right where he said he'd be, although he never mentioned being naked and aroused. Dark hair curled in the middle of his chest. His muscled arms with their popping veins put romantic novel cover models to shame. "Are you trying to shock or surprise me?"

"If you're surprised, I'm doing something wrong." He nuzzled her neck as he unbuttoned her blue-and-white striped camp shirt.

"Not wrong."

The loose-fitting garment fell to the floor.

She should stop him. But the way his mouth massaged her skin, tongue lapping as if nectar coated her body, weakened her resolve. Her bra joined her shirt. His calloused palms cupped her breasts, thumbs gently flicking her nipples. He nudged her toward the bed.

The mattress edge hit the back of her thighs. Her knees were too wobbly to support her. She collapsed.

He stretched out next to her and pulled her onto her back. "Do you trust me?" He flitted his fingers across her breasts.

"Yes." She spoke without hesitation, without giving credence to her earlier dark musings. She had to trust him. Otherwise, she couldn't trust herself.

He leaned over her, his gaze dark and intense. "Would you trust me enough to let me handcuff you to the headboard and make love to you?" He unzipped her fly and brushed the pads of his fingers across the bared flesh below her navel. "Please."

She hesitated. Closed her eyes to prevent him from distracting her.

Trust. She'd trusted him well enough the previous evening. Trusted him enough to stay with him. The handcuffs were too kinky for her comfort level, but what she understood about intimacy could fit in the gap in a link of the chain binding the cuffs together.

Except she didn't like how he'd made trust into something that mattered only when he had control. She refused to let sex make her stupid.

Trust worked both ways. He needed to trust her, too.

She opened her eyes as she crossed her arms to hide her bare breasts. Okay, yesterday, when he'd mentioned illegal tactics, she'd imagined him tying her to his bed. The reality didn't sit well. "We never discussed bondage."

"Bondage? No. Your pleasure." He lifted his eyes to meet hers and stroked her arm.

His fingers were hot as branding irons against her skin.

"We never discussed anything about sex, not even your virginity."

Oh yeah. Good point. Still, there was an enormous difference between the missionary position and getting kinky.

"Your inexperience excites me and makes me fantasize about all the different ways I want to make love to you. I want to help you explore your sexuality."

She inhaled to calm herself. How could he respect her boundaries when she'd never defined them, even for herself?

"Do you usually chain women to your bed?"

"No." His mesmerizing focus nearly paralyzed her.

"Then why the handcuffs?"

"So you won't try to touch me while I make love to you. I want you to focus only on how good I can make you feel, not reciprocating the pleasure."

She believed him. His stated motive made sense, but the idea of handcuffs still bothered her. Maybe someday she could consent to them, but not this early in their relationship. Not until she understood the specifics.

"Compromise," she whispered.

He cocked his head. "How?"

She studied his iron headboard. The simple design gave her an idea. She might not be ready for manacles, but she could pretend. Simulate.

"What if I—" It felt as if half the peeper population had immigrated from the pond to her throat. Plus, her exposed breasts embarrassed her. Maybe she'd be more comfortable being partially naked with a man after a decade or two. She wanted to know what had prompted Cam to try handcuffs. Not curious enough to let him shackle her, but enough to quash her modesty.

She stretched out on the mattress. "Do you trust me?" she croaked.

"Yes." He answered without hesitation.

She stretched her arms and grasped the posts on the headboard.

Cam's lips trembled. "I swear I will not hurt you. I am not into pain. But you have to promise not to let go. No matter what."

She nodded.

"Say it," he urged, as he leaned over her.

"I promise not to let go, no matter what."

His sweet kiss sealed their deal. Gently. Thoroughly.

Not enough. She wanted to be consumed by him.

Slowly, as if reading her mind, his mouth became more aggressive. His hands became involved, fingers lightly stroking the side of her neck. Her throat.

She wanted to touch him, to curl her fingers into his shoulders or trace the whorls of black ink decorating his shoulders and biceps.

As if reading her mind, Cam slid his hands up her arms, past her wrists, until his palms wrapped lightly around her fingers, reminding her of her promise.

She shivered as his tongue traced her ear's outer rim, then bit the lobe before nibbling his way down the side of her neck. Closing her eyes, she sank into the sensations.

At some point, her legs splayed, and Cam fit himself between her thighs. But not in the way she expected. His chest rested on her belly as he lavished attention on her breasts. His hands joined his mouth. Not rushing his touches as he'd done the previous evening but taking time to explore every millimeter of her more-than-generous body.

She never knew the human tongue could reshape itself in so many configurations; that a man's lips could be so pliable, soft, yet strong and firm at the same time. No one had ever tested how sensitive her breasts could be. To her, they'd been appendages on her chest, getting in her way and acting as a shelf for collecting spilled food. Cam's caresses sparked reactions deep inside her.

"Cam." She didn't know if she gasped or moaned.

He nipped the inside curve of her left breast, then licked away the sting.

If he didn't touch her lower, more intimately, she would go mad, and she told him so.

He ignored her.

Well, he hadn't lied when he told her he liked foreplay and kissing.

Darby was soft. Not only her skin—and Cam worried his callouses and the stubble on his face would scratch her—but everywhere. Exactly as he'd imagined she would be when he first met her. Soft, comfortable, delectable. No woman had ever tasted as delicious on his tongue. Her tits were the finest he'd ever been lucky enough to fondle or feast upon, with nipples puckered as tight as the wild blackcaps growing in the mountains.

He would gladly stay in their neighborhood forever.

But Darby's squirming distracted him. He'd heard some women could orgasm through nipple stimulation alone. Darby's reactions sparked his curiosity. But not tonight. In the end, how she climaxed didn't matter as long as he satisfied her. If he accomplished nothing else in his life, he was determined to pleasure Darby in any and every way he could.

"Lift your hips." He needed to rid her of her jeans. He'd already unfastened the waist and lowered the zipper. He needed only to tug the snug denim over her ass, down her legs, and off her feet.

She reached for him.

"Uh-uh," he reminded her. "Hands on the headboard."

She complied, and her jeans and panties soon joined her shirt and bra on the floor.

The scent of her arousal filled the room. Filled all the empty spaces in his head. His body. His soul.

He licked his way south, sliding his body lower as he headed for ground zero.

Her belly quivered.

"Cam, no," she said.

"Do you really want me to stop?" He could barely get the words out.

"I want you inside of me." Half pant, half moan.

"You're too tender, and there's more than one way I can make love to you. If you'll let me." He slid a finger into her wetness. "Please don't ask me to stop."

She flinched.

She was more sensitive than any woman he'd ever touched. All her nerve endings languished on her surface, waiting for him to awaken them. The idea empowered him. He traced her navel with his tongue.

"Okay." Barely more than a whisper. A breath of consent.

He slid lower and hoisted her legs over his shoulders.

Darby whimpered.

He cupped her ass in his hands and blew on the tangled nest of wiry hair marking her spot like an X on a treasure map. Sniffed the thatch, savoring her aroma and reveling in the decidedly old-fash-ioned delight that no other man had ever been as privileged.

He dove in.

Darby's arms ached. Her fingers cramped from where she'd grabbed the bars on the headboard. Yet if she hadn't grasped them, she might have levitated off the bed. Soared beyond the ceiling. Now she was limp. Not only could she not move her arms, but every muscle in her body was incapable of reacting.

Cam lay beside her, his body radiating heat. "You okay?" His erection prodded her thigh.

She summoned the strength to answer. "Ask me again tomorrow. What about you?"

"I'll be fine."

"Doesn't seem fair." He'd done all the work. He'd earned a payback.

"Then you'll have to make it up to me. But later."

She tried to hold back her sigh of relief. Not only did she not have the strength to reciprocate, but she also wouldn't know what to do. Oh, she'd read enough to grasp oral sex basics—thanks to her teenaged-self purloining her grandmother's romance novels—but whatever she attempted would not match the mouth-magic Cam had worked on her. His performance far exceeded her imagination.

"I'll put 'payback' on my list for tomorrow," Darby murmured. Sensation in her fingers slowly returned. She used one to trace the tattoos on his shoulder, too wrung out to ask him what the patterns inked into his skin meant. Something else for tomorrow.

"What else is on your list?" Cam asked.

"Laundry. At least I don't have to use the laundromat anymore. There's a washer and dryer at Nippletop. I still need to buy pepper spray and should visit my folks. Pack my stuff." Her voice faded as her energy waned. Her eyelids grew heavy.

"Do your laundry here," Cam offered. "Makes no sense to trek to the camp when everything else is right in Saranac Lake."

"My folks are in Wilmington," she reminded him. "I want to borrow my dad's 12 gauge."

"I would rather you didn't arm yourself with a gun, especially a shotgun." Cam rolled onto his side. "Hey, look at me."

She opened her eyes. His sharp gaze warned her he planned a serious conversation.

"If you're going to use a gun, a handgun would be better for your purposes. That's not going to happen anytime soon, unless you have a pistol permit you haven't mentioned."

"But—"

"Think about it, Darby," Cam interrupted her. "You can't keep a shotgun at hand. You're better off sticking with OC spray that you can carry in your pocket. And a tube is a lot more difficult to wrestle away from you than a 12-gauge would be. I'm guessing your dad's shotgun is standard and holds only three shells, so if you're trying to defend yourself, you'd better be a damn good shot. If you can get to it in time."

Cam's logical brain irritated her. She prided herself on her methodical ways, her calm when faced with chaos. Dysfunction didn't intimidate her, yet Cam made her feel like a helpless, dust-bunny-brained female—all the negative self-imagery she'd believed James Coolidge Astin's bequest had banished.

She closed her eyes. Damn it. Cam had a point. He always had a point.

"Fine," she huffed. "No shotgun, and I'll do my laundry here."

"What are our revised plans for tomorrow?"

If Cam didn't stop talking, she wouldn't get her nap. Wasn't there a cliché about men falling asleep right after sex? Except he hadn't climaxed. She'd have to remedy the lack if for no other reason than to make him hush so she could get sleep.

Besides, she was curious.

They'd spent their naked time focused on her, especially after Cam discovered he'd been her first. She'd been content to wallow in his attention. He needed a turn.

"I need to pack." She placed her palm flat against his belly.

His muscles tensed.

"I want the boxes of my things ready to go once parts of the lodge are cleaned out." She slid her hand lower. "The dumpster is coming next Tuesday morning, so I have a week to cull the… junk from the… jewels."

She brushed her fingers along his swelling penis, fascinated by how an erection happened. The textures intrigued her; how the veins and tissues beneath the smooth skin shaped the structure. Different from the wiry-haired skin covering his abs.

"Darby."

His voice held a warning. Or perhaps a plea.

Within seconds, she realized she would need both hands to fully investigate him.

She opened her eyes to find his luminous gaze fixed on her. Then he closed his eyes, as if yielding to the sensations her explorations evoked.

She paid attention to his face, the twitches and expressions, how this touch resulted in that response. Which caresses pleased him best.

He took her hand and wrapped her fingers around him. Guided her into stroking instead of fondling. He adjusted her other hand until her palm cradled his testicles.

Once she'd settled into the rhythm he preferred, he released her hands in order to cup her face. Kiss her.

Her first instinct was to recoil. She knew where his mouth had been, but she forgot her hesitation as his tongue brushed hers. The scent and taste she'd left behind weren't as repugnant as she'd feared. She focused on him. Thus far, she'd been doing all the taking, sexually speaking. She wanted to love him as well as he loved her. To be as giving. As aware.

Listening to the changes in Cam's respiration, counting the beats of his heart against her bare breasts, and cataloging every twitch, pulse, and spasm obsessed her.

He stopped kissing her, jerked upright, and grabbed the tissue box from the bedside table. His shuddering jostled the bed.

She studied his face as he climaxed. For a moment, she worried he might be in pain. His expression resembled a grimace, with his closed eyes and lowered brow, dropped jaw and parted lips.

He collapsed next to her, his chest heaving as he sucked in oxygen. "What happened to tomorrow?" he wheezed.

"I decided you needed help to go to sleep," she confessed.

"You're a wicked woman."

She closed her eyes and smiled. "Don't you forget it."

CHAPTER TEN

WEDNESDAY, JUNE 14, 2000

C am checked the eggs in the frying pan. He'd pulled break-fast duty while Darby showered. The scents of sizzling bacon and brewing coffee pervaded the room. He didn't have the greatest kitchen, but he didn't require a gourmet set-up. Darby's apartment barely qualified as cook friendly. The camp kitchen defied description. He shuddered when he tried to envision flipping pancakes at the over-sized black monstrosity of a gas stove he'd seen during yesterday's tour. He hoped the trust fund contained enough for extensive rehabbing.

After glancing out the window, he reconsidered eating breakfast on the deck. The rain-laden clouds appeared ready to burst open. Today would be the perfect day to go shopping. Darby could get her defense spray, and he needed to buy a few items for his peace of mind.

He was so lost in thought that when she slid her arms around his waist and rested her cheek on his back, she startled him. "I'll finish here while you shower," she offered.

He would have preferred showering together but surrendered to her plea for privacy. Once he stood beneath the jet and soaped his body, he mentally conceded she'd been right. Like she'd been right about too much time together too fast. He had two more days off come the weekend, but Darby worked every weekend. Until she quit the diner, the only time their schedules would mesh would be every other Tuesday and Wednesday. She'd never mentioned her future employment at Chuck's Local Diner.

At least Red Beard couldn't get her at the Local.

The rain held off until they were on their second cups of coffee. Even then, Darby stayed on the deck.

"I love summer rain," she said, when she sought shelter in the kitchen. Her camp shirt, patterned with vividly colored flowers and searing yellow suns, provided a counterpoint to the gloom outside the window.

"Easy to say when you aren't out in it." Rain made his job more difficult, especially when someone lost their way in the wilderness. Slogging through mud sucked. And unless Mother Nature provided a heavy downpour, mosquitos and other biting insects didn't relent in their quest for food. Rain only sloughed off the insect repellent applied to exposed skin.

"I'm not made of sugar," she reminded him. "I won't melt."

"What say we hit the Walmart in Plattsburgh?" he asked, as he loaded their eggy plates in the dishwasher. "You can get your OC spray, and we can lay in some supplies."

"Okay."

The trip required the morning and most of the afternoon. The drive alone took an hour and a half each way. Easy conversation filled the time. Darby asked questions, and Cam answered. She inquired about matters that would appear once they were married—religion, politics, and which way to hang the toilet paper. They meshed on every essential level, with similar beliefs and habits.

He especially loved her questions regarding his favorite superhero. His was unusual. Captain Planet, the environmentalist superhero.

They found their only sticking point when discussing what to name their sons.

"If we get married," she qualified.

"When." He considered it a win for not clenching his teeth as he corrected her.

"And if I decide to take your name—"

"Why wouldn't you change your name to mine?"

She continued as if he hadn't interrupted. "Then we'll name our first son Remington. If I don't take your last name, we'll negotiate what to call the boys."

"Negotiating could be fun." His thoughts flashed back to the previous evening. They'd been able to bargain a mutually satisfying conclusion.

Darby's cheeks flushed as pink as the flowers printed on her shirt. "Not to mention fulfilling." She cleared her throat. "Chicken. White meat or dark? Boneless or bone in?"

"I'm glad you suggested shopping," Darby said, as she hopped from Cam's SUV to Walmart's parking lot. The smell of wet blacktop clung to the humid air. "I like rain, but not driving in it."

She'd written a shopping list, but she'd left her notebook at Cam's place. Her priority was defense spray, but that's all she remembered.

She couldn't buy linens and such for the retreat yet. Besides, she wanted something more upscale than discount bedding and towels. She planned to charge writers a mint for the opportunity to isolate themselves from the world in order to work. She needed to make the cost worth their while. But cleaning supplies and groceries? Time to stock up.

After they'd each purchased the maximum amount of OC spray allowed by New York State law—two devices containing point 75 ounces each—Cam and Darby split up. He had his priorities, and she had hers.

He didn't need to know what feminine hygiene products she used.

Damn. She'd forgotten to call Planned Parenthood. She and Cam could joke about naming their potential children, but she did not need an oopsie pregnancy. All her attention needed to be on transforming Camp Nippletop into The Write Place.

She'd snooped in his cupboards and fridge while he'd showered to learn what he liked to eat and what provisions he kept on hand. They weren't married yet. He could restock his own supplies. But there were other items she could purchase, such as ingredients for meals. Her natural thriftiness rebelled against eating out every night. A pizza once in a while, okay, but her inherent frugality refused to indulge regularly.

They checked out separately and met at the front of the store. Darby waited with their carts while Cam drove his SUV to the loading area. The rain had stopped, but humidity still burdened the air.

Darby had latched her seatbelt when Cam extended a key. "To my house."

She hesitated before taking it.

"You're the first woman I've ever given a key to," he said, his eyes fixed on hers.

She did not have spare keys to her camp or her apartment and didn't plan to have extras made for Cam. Swapping keys bothered her because the exchange symbolized... a promise. A contract. An assumption of an agreement she hadn't made.

Did he expect her to give him access to her spaces?

"Thank you." Having access to his house made sense, since she was staying with him, although her landlord had replaced the broken locks at her apartment.

Besides, possessing a key didn't mean she had to use it.

"Want to stop for lunch before we head home?" Cam asked.

"Not especially. The chicken I bought needs to be refrigerated."

"Good point."

Darby relaxed in her seat, lulled by the hiss of tires on the still-wet pavement. Cam didn't turn on the radio. Darby appreciated the quiet. Noise filled her days at the diner: customers chattering, flatware clattering against dishes, and food sizzling on the grill. Sometimes a girl needed silence.

As if reading her mind, Cam asked, "When do you need to be at work tomorrow?"

"Five-thirty." Since she lived only a few blocks from the Local, she'd never figured commuting into her morning routine. Staying with Cam meant changes. Timing would become a bigger issue when she lived at the camp. She imagined the drive from Nippletop to Saranac Lake in sub-zero winter morning darkness and wanted to weep.

"How much longer do you plan to work at the diner?" He switched on the wipers as they drove through a tunnel of trees. Droplets fell from the overhead leaves.

"I need to keep working. I have bills." Well, not rent if she continued to stay with Cam until the move to the camp. But car payments, gas, insurance—those expenses weren't going to take care of themselves. And if she remained at Cam's cabin, she would pay her fair share. Like the groceries she'd purchased. She paid her own way.

"Can't you draw a salary from the trust fund?"

She twisted in her seat to look at him. "What?"

"If you have only a year to get the retreat open, you need to spend all your time on that instead of squeezing the work around another job."

"This is an about face from you," she said.

She noticed his jaw tighten as if he clenched his teeth.

"Well, yeah. But it's what you want, and I don't want you wearing yourself out working two full-time jobs." His thumbs on the steering wheel tapped out a counter-rhythm to the thump of the wipers. "Getting the lodge alone in shape, even if you're only overseeing sub-contracted workers, is going to be a massive undertaking."

Subcontracted workers? A salary for herself? Why hadn't Howard Chatham made these suggestions?

The road emerged from the trees. The sky revealed deep blue shards as the gray cloud cover fractured.

"I'm not happy you're alone there so much," he admitted. "But you have your OC spray. I bought a pack for you, too. Promise me you'll always keep at least one can on you."

"Okay."

"Say it."

"I promise I will always keep pepper spray on me. Cross my heart and hope to die. Give me your hand, and I'll pinky swear."

He shocked her by taking his hand off the steering wheel and extending it toward her.

She hooked her little finger into his. "I will keep my pepper spray on me all the time."

The road twisted again. Cam drove into a patch of brilliant sunlight. And there, curving in the sky ahead of them, a double rainbow arced across the horizon.

"Let's take a ride out to your camp," Cam suggested once they'd unloaded their purchases.

Darby had bought food. He'd laid in supplies for his lunches. Luckily, most of his purchases were shelf stable. She'd filled his refrigerator with vegetables and fruits. She'd barely left space for the case of Moonsinger he'd picked up.

But he'd splurged on something else.

Things didn't normally excite him. Darby changed that. He could barely contain himself thinking about what he'd bought. The last time he'd been this antsy was when he was five, and he and his siblings had roused their parents at four on Christmas morning to see if Santa had visited.

He had a present for Darby. A gift. A promise to show her he accepted her entrepreneurship. That he respected her goals and ambition. At least, he hoped she'd see the gift that way. She hadn't been thrilled when he gave her the key to his house, which had been a gigantic step for him.

He reminded himself what she'd said to him their first night together: *I wanted you to act as if we've been lovers for weeks. Months. Years.* He considered her words a promise.

She was puttering around his kitchen, muttering *chicken, marinade,* and *grill,* when he suggested they drive out to The Write Place.

"I'd rather go into Saranac Lake and grab my laundry and do some packing."

Her suggestion made more sense, except his surprise was for the camp, not her apartment. But he had promised her laundry facilities.

"Okay," he agreed. "We can pick up subs for dinner while we're in town."

"No," Darby said. "We're having chicken for dinner. You have a grill, and we should use it. I assume you've filled your propane tank for the season."

He pretended to be insulted. "I'm a guy, aren't I?"

"You certainly are. Thank goodness. Let me get my keys—I'll drive this time."

He opened his mouth to protest, but she cut him off.

"I want to pack a couple of boxes and take them to the camp tomorrow after work. Loading my Jeep tonight while you're with me to help carry the boxes downstairs makes more sense than waiting until tomorrow."

He couldn't argue with her logic. She planned to go to Nippletop after she got off work the next day. He understood why. Daylight hours were at their longest. She could accomplish a lot. She was armed with defense spray.

Dread still coiled like a viper inside him.

"What time do you think you'll be at the camp tomorrow?" He tried to be nonchalant despite the knots in his gut.

"I get out at three," she said, as she tucked a tube of OC spray in her front pocket. She winked at him. "On me at all times."

"Thank you."

She seemed surprised by his response. "Hey." She wrapped her arms around his waist. "I realize I worry you, and I love your concern."

She didn't love him but loved that he worried about her. Great. Chuck, who owned the diner where she worked, probably worried about her, too.

She released Cam before the casual embrace morphed into something more.

Right. They needed to get going.

He didn't speak again until they were on the road. "I could arrange my workday to meet you at the camp around three-thirty, four o'clock, barring an emergency."

His job allowed him to set his own hours. He could adjust his plans for the following day. He frequently spent sunrise hours on the weekends at various trailheads to instruct visitors about the dos and don'ts of High Peak hiking. Tourists sometimes arrived on a Thursday for a long weekend. He could make it work.

"Thank you," Darby replied. "I'm not as jittery when I'm not alone."

Maybe he should get her a dog. Not a puppy, but a big German shepherd or some other breed of guard dog.

Cam helped her carry boxes partially filled with newspapers to her apartment.

"I won't be long," she promised. "I need to get my laundry together, pack a few cupboards."

He started wrapping plates in the newspapers and stacking them in a box. Being idle when there was work to do wasn't in his makeup. He'd emptied one shelf when she joined him in her kitchen. "You don't need to pitch in, but thanks."

"No worries. Where did you get all the newspapers?"

"Freebies from the diner's foyer." She grabbed a Hellmann's Mayonnaise box and headed toward another cupboard.

"I don't know why I kept all these coffee mugs," she grumbled. "When I moved out on my own, everyone in the family gave me every promotional cup they'd ever received, and I was too ignorant to say, 'no thank you'."

"Do you need to take them all? You could leave the castoffs and your landlord could rent the place as partially furnished. I have more than enough for us. Everyone gives them away nowadays."

She pulled a mug from the cupboard and wrapped it. "I have favorites," she confessed, "but yeah, you make a good point. I should save what I want and donate the rest to Goodwill. I swear, these things reproduce like guppies."

Cam snorted.

"Oh. I'd hoped I kept this," she said a minute later.

Cam glanced up from wrapping a bowl.

She extended a mug toward him. "For you."

Cam recognized the blue face immediately, even without reading the character's name on the mug. "Captain Planet."

"The Power is Yours," she quoted, as she flipped the mug so he could read the slogan printed opposite the captain's face. "You said he was your favorite superhero growing up."

Cam didn't know what to say. He took the cup from her and studied the artwork. Captain Planet and the Planeteers were part of the reason he'd become a forest ranger. To protect and preserve the earth's natural resources.

As much as he'd loved the cartoon, he'd never had promotional swag. Other kids carried Superman or Spiderman backpacks and wore sweatshirts emblazoned with Marvel or DC logos. He'd had nothing. Until this woman, this amazing creature with whom he wanted to build a future, had given him something he hadn't realized he'd been missing from his past.

He swallowed around the Whiteface-Mountain-sized lump clogging his throat.

"My mom got it at a yard sale," Darby said. "She liked the periwinkle interior."

She must mean the purplish-blue glaze on the inside.

"It's a nice color," he managed to rasp out.

"If you don't want it, I can donate it—"

"No!" He lifted his eyes from the mug as he tightened his grip on the handle.

Confusion masked Darby's face.

"No," he said in a calmer tone. "It's mine. Thank you."

He carefully set the mug on the counter. Then he wrapped his arms around Darby. She fit perfectly against him. He lowered his face and brushed his lips against hers. It might have been the first time in his adult life he kissed a non-blood relative woman without being motivated by sex. Darby was turning him inside out.

He would wait for her forever.

CHAPTER ELEVEN

THURSDAY, JUNE 15, 2000

Darby unlocked the door to the main lodge at The Write Place. She'd arrived before Cam, which didn't surprise her. She worked a set schedule at the diner. Being a forest ranger meant a fluid workday. For all she knew, she might not see him until the next day. She needed to get used to being flexible, not only for him but also for being an innkeeper.

She had a few phone calls to make before she poked around in the outbuildings. Sitting in Astin's worn-out leather chair at his massive and cluttered desk, she called the women's health clinic in Saranac Lake first. She wanted to get the most personal call done before Cam arrived. Yes, they shared birth control responsibility. But her natural reticence regarding sex—the logic behind her not telling Cam she'd been a virgin—demanded privacy for that phone call.

After she'd made an appointment, she called Howard Chatham, Astin's attorney. Well, her attorney. She doubted she would ever be used to being a person who retained an attorney and an accountant.

Having a lover dazed her. No wonder half the time she stumbled around as if in a dream. Only her shift at the diner felt real anymore.

She had no idea how much of a salary she should request. She should have discussed it with Cam.

Her breath caught. Discuss her salary with Cam? She hadn't known the man a week, yet he'd become her touchstone. Which was crazy.

She could figure this out by herself. She needed at least enough money to match what she made at the Local, including tips. While she wouldn't have the expense of rent and the trust handled the utilities, she'd be using more gas and paying for more meals. Hopefully the trade-off would be even. And if it wasn't? She'd ask Chatham to make an adjustment.

She wasn't comfortable bringing up the points Cam had suggested, but she did it anyway. *I need a salary for my work on opening the retreat. I need to hire subcontractors to get things moving.*

After disconnecting, she stared at the thick layer of dust covering the bookshelves like mangy gray fur. She didn't have to tackle the cleaning. She could hire a service to come in and do the heavy lifting. *James' former housekeeper might be available,* Chatham had advised her. *I'm sure Tara Nolan would be happy for the work.* He provided the woman's phone number.

As far as her own salary? Chatham had suggested an amount that was twice what she earned at the diner, even if everyone tipped her twenty-five percent. Darby hadn't argued.

Architect, cleaners, housekeeper, give her notice at the Local. Her hand trembled as she wrote the new list in her notebook. Forward progress. She could do this.

She exhaled the breath she hadn't realized she'd been holding and pushed away from the desk. The stuffiness of the library gave her a headache. She'd been stuck in the diner for hours. Fresh air might clear the cobwebs from her brain.

She checked her pockets for her keys and her defense spray. All set. She let herself out the French doors at the back of the great room.

The wide veranda overlooked Nippletop Lake and begged for furniture. She vaguely recalled glimpsing wicker during her initial tour with Chatham. Maybe she didn't have a nice deck like Cam, but she owned an old-fashioned porch. She could use the space as a warm-weather sanctuary.

She made her way across the overgrown lawn and realized she should have asked Chatham about a groundskeeper. The tall grass provided the perfect breeding ground for deer ticks. At least she'd been smart enough to wear jeans and sneakers, despite the warm day.

A rusty padlock secured the boathouse door. She took her ring of keys and began trying them. Lucky number seven. The lock needed WD40, and she struggled with the shackle until it opened. She needed to put buying a new combination lock on her list.

She should have brought the notebook with her.

The door creaked open. The dark, dank interior smelled like lake water. She shuddered and hoped no creatures lurked inside. Especially snakes. She didn't like rodents or spiders any better, but mammals and arachnids didn't creep her out the way reptiles did.

Light dribbled in through small dusty windows positioned near the rafters. Lacy webs curtained the glass panes. Water lapped against the edges of the worn wood flooring surrounding the empty slip. The loft containing wicker porch furniture wasn't in the boathouse.

She turned to leave.

A tall shadow loomed in the doorway. She shrieked, dropped her keys, and fumbled for the pepper spray wedged in her jeans pocket.

"Whoa," Cam said, catching her upper arms.

"You scared the snot out me." And maybe her heart, judging by the rapid thudding in her chest. "What the heck, Captain Planet? You're lucky I didn't spray you."

She jerked free and bent over, trying to catch her breath. Screaming had used all the air in her lungs.

Cam scooped her key ring from the ground. "You didn't hear me pull in or calling for you? What are you doing out here?"

She straightened and snatched her keys from him. "Looking for porch furniture. I remember spotting some when Chatham took me around. It must be somewhere else."

Cam entered the boathouse and looked around. "Holy shit."

"What? A snake?" Darby took a step back. Good thing Cam still wore his uniform, including his sidearm. She could not deal with a snake.

"Is that what I think it is?" His deep voice echoed in the empty building.

"Shoot it," she advised.

A beam of light pierced the gloom. She peeked inside.

He'd pulled his flashlight from his duty belt and used it to study the rafters. "Do you know what's hanging up there?" he asked in a hushed tone.

She peered toward the item she'd missed, suspended in the shadows. Now, in the brightness of Cam's light, she saw an elongated dust-covered shape. But beneath the dirty film, she recognized wood grain. "An old canoe?"

"Oh, man. What a beauty. And it's yours?" He played the beam along the length of the boat.

"Um, yeah. I guess." She didn't remember a canoe on the inventory, but she could double check. "But if it's been unused for years, it's probably rotted."

"Maybe, maybe not. Whoever stored it did a good job. I won't be able to tell until I can bring it down. From here, it looks like it only needs a little TLC."

Darby blinked. Something at Camp Nippletop excited Cam? She must have wandered into an alternate universe.

"Would you mind if I came out on Saturday while you're at work and took a closer look?"

He continued to confuse her. She thought he hated the camp.

"You're off on Saturday?"

"I work every other weekend and have every second Tuesday and Wednesday off." He spoke as if not paying attention to what he said, his focus entirely on the canoe.

"Knock yourself out." She certainly wasn't going to haul it down herself.

He turned off his flashlight and grinned at her. "You're going to keep it, right?"

She didn't understand his enthusiasm, but what was that saying about beauty being in the eye of the beholder? "Unless the wood is so far gone, it's only good for kindling."

"Nah. I'll restore it."

"You know how to restore a canoe?"

"Nope. But I can learn. It will make a great project."

"The estate could pay to refurbish it. What's the point in having a trust if I don't use it?" She paraphrased Chatham.

The lawyer had assured her that as long as the funds in the trust were being used to turn the camp into a retreat there would be no problem. The canoe could be used by writers needing to . . . she had no idea what authors actually did, other than write books and eat breakfast at greasy spoon diners.

One more thing for her to learn. But she could learn.

"I'd rather restore it myself. If you don't mind."

At least he asked permission.

"Anyway, let's get this beauty locked up," he said, as he fastened the padlock. "You're looking for furniture?"

"I remember seeing wicker chairs. If the furniture is usable, I can put it out on the veranda."

"Veranda?" He raised an eyebrow.

"If I'm changing the camp into a high-end retreat, I need to use high end language to describe it."

He laughed. "Sounds good. By the way, you need a new lock. This one's too rusty to be secure."

"I noticed. I thought I'd replace it with a combination lock. Then you wouldn't need a key to access the canoe." She was thinking long-term with him when she had no business doing so.

"You might want to consider a key-pad lock system. Everywhere," Cam suggested as they strolled toward the main lodge. "Then you wouldn't have to worry about guests losing keys. You can change the codes after every check out."

Something else for her list. "You are scathingly brilliant. What would I do without you?"

"I hope you never have to find out. By the way, I bought something for you yesterday."

"More condoms?" He'd already given her the key to his place in Ray Brook and two tubes of pepper spray. She hoped he hadn't purchased a ring. She wasn't ready for a ring.

He squeezed her butt. "Nope. Something for the camp, really. And, selfishly, for my peace of mind."

"Condoms don't give you peace of mind?"

He snorted. "Let's just say I don't have nightmares about getting you pregnant. All that would mean is we start our family sooner than we'd planned."

They'd reached Astin's office before she could tell him about her appointment for birth control. Then a box printed with pictures of telephones sitting on the desk further distracted her.

Okay. A ring she could accept.

"It's a cordless phone system. I'll replace the base unit here, then you'll have four cordless extensions to use around the property. You can carry one around with you all the time. In case you need to call for help."

He didn't wait for her reaction to unpack the phones.

"Any other extension can stay," he continued. "The charging bases for the portables need power outlets. Think about where you want them."

Her brain blanked. She didn't know what to say. The phones were an incredibly thoughtful purchase. She never would have considered something like cordless phones. Gadgets and gizmos were outside her experience. Change happened slowly in the north country. To her.

But change figured in to why Astin left his property to her. He'd seen in her a willingness to stretch her mind and accept new ideas. After all, she'd read his books. And told him she had, not to suck up to him for bigger tips, but because she'd enjoyed the stories.

If she hadn't inherited the camp, she might not have met Cam. He'd definitely expanded her horizons. If for no other reason, she ought to put flowers on Astin's grave.

Styrofoam squealed as Cam unboxed the phones. Static-filled pebbles of the stuff clung like magnetic snow to his big, capable hands.

"I need to grab the pre-set speed dial numbers off Astin's phone." She strolled around the desk. Anything to keep from fantasizing—oh, heck, remembering—the magic Cam's fingers performed. "Especially Chatham's."

"I can program the numbers into the new base," Cam said. "Along with my cell phone and 9-1-1."

Swapping out the phones took next to no time. Unplug the old, 1980s version and snap in the new. Then they searched the lodge together, deciding on placement for the four new extensions. When they entered Astin's former bedroom on the second floor, Cam looked around with more interest than he'd shown before. The phone extension on the night table did not need replacing.

"Is this where you intended to stay until your living quarters are ready?" He spoke in the past tense, as if her plans had changed, that she would be spending every night with him until the rehab was complete.

"Yeah. Astin was in High Peaks Hospice when he passed. But there's something creepy about using his sheets. I don't know if his housekeeper changed them after he went into hospice or..." She shuddered. "I should have bought new bed linens at Wal-Mart yesterday."

"Then we won't christen the bed today."

"Ew, no." She narrowed her eyes. Cam's uniform made him look sexier than usual. Hot. Jumpable. Not that she'd ever jumped a man in her life, but first times defined her relationship with Cam. He wasn't shy about wanting to have sex with her. Why not now?

"The rug?" He sounded hopeful.

She shifted her attention to the intricately patterned dark red wool. Who knew the last time someone ran a vacuum? "Nope."

"I know." He snapped his fingers. "The desk in the office. You said you wanted to convert it into a game room. Let's play in there."

He grabbed her hand and tugged her into the hall.

"Do you have a condom?" she asked, between giggles, as he led her down the stairs.

"Since meeting you, I pack at least three."

"You won't be inconvenienced much longer. I made an appointment at the clinic." The words were easy to say while he was in such a playful mood.

"Even better than finding the canoe." He pulled her across the great room. "Almost as good as meeting you."

She hadn't seen this side of Cam before. He acted lighthearted. Even when they teased each other, he usually exuded an underlying intensity. She hadn't acknowledged the weight of his moods until now.

Could she live with someone who rarely relaxed?

More importantly, could she live without him?

Could he ever get enough of this woman?

For the first time in his life, Cam understood the afterglow.

He could swear his bones had wandered off, maybe to swim in the lake. All he wanted was to cuddle with Darby, but the surface of James Coolidge Astin's desk didn't invite snuggling. Still, Cam couldn't move, not until his bones returned. Until his muscles stopped pulsing. Until oxygen saturated his brain.

Maybe making love on the desk hadn't been a great idea, but Darby nixed the unstable leather chair.

Until he recovered, he rested between her splayed thighs and nuzzled her neck. Her skin tasted salty, and she smelled like french fries, perspiration, and his balsam soap.

They'd christened the future game room. How many other rooms in the lodge required his attention? Outbuildings? How awkward would making love to Darby in the old wooden canoe be? Cam needed to create new memories, to put his stamp on the atmosphere, banish Astin and Red Beard, and make The Write Place his place. Their place.

Meeting Darby had narrowed his world. Unfamiliar emotions had filled his first day back at work since they'd gotten together. He didn't have words to identify his emotions, although he tried while he patrolled his territory. Luckily, no overdue hikers or injuries on a mountain required his attention. He'd found no meth labs, marijuana fields, or paramilitary training grounds, only black flies, mosquitos, and a shy gray fox family. And time to muse. Lots of time to muse.

Because Darby filled his mind. How her smile used her entire face. The weight of her breasts in his hands. The sounds she made as he thrust into her. All the ways she tried to take care of him, like the bits of grilled chicken he'd packed for his lunch.

It boggled his mind that their first date had been only three nights ago. He couldn't remember life before her and couldn't picture a future without her.

Chapter Twelve

"Well, that was special," Darby quipped, as she tucked her breasts into her bra.

Cam rearranged his own parts. "One room down, how many to go?" Laying claim to the Great Camp might be more fun than he'd expected.

"I don't know." Darby didn't sound concerned. "Should we count them?"

"You don't have a room-by-room breakdown in your notebook?" he teased. "Shocking."

"I haven't counted the outbuildings, either. I swear I'm always stumbling across ones I've never seen before. Maybe we should explore to see if one is worth converting into living quarters."

He noticed she didn't say "our home," although she'd included him in the decision process. "Sure."

The sun wouldn't set for another couple of hours, giving them time to explore.

They followed an overgrown path along the edge of the lake.

"Where's your property line?" Cam asked, after watching Darby map several buildings in a rough sketch.

"I'm not sure," she admitted. "I own the lake and the land around it for roughly a mile in every direction. Park wilderness fully surrounds the property. I heard a rumor the state made Astin remove his 'trespassers will be shot' postings."

"Is the property otherwise posted?"

"I think so. Astin was a recluse and didn't want hunters, snowmobilers, or campers wandering around."

Cam should have noticed when he investigated after Red Beard's visit. "Even if Astin did post signs, you'll need to update them with your name and address."

She jotted his advice in her notebook.

"That could be the old icehouse," Darby murmured a few moments later. She pointed at a small building tucked into a thick copse of balsam firs near the lakeshore. "I don't remember Chatham bringing me this far, but he mentioned the property included an icehouse."

"This must be it," Cam said. "What will you do with it?"

"No clue." Darby stumbled on a branch lying in the path.

Cam caught her arm to keep her from falling. "You should wear boots, not sneakers."

"I'll add a pair to my shopping list."

Her chilly tone surprised him. He wondered what was wrong, especially when she didn't make a note of his suggestion.

As they drew closer to the building, Cam observed wide, double doors facing the lake, used for hauling ice blocks into storage. A heavy-duty black padlock secured another door on the backside.

"That lock looks new," Darby said.

Cam didn't care for the implication. "I don't suppose you have a key."

"My keys are ancient. Let's check them out."

He put out his arm to stop her from going any closer to the building. "Wait here, in case the path or icehouse is boobytrapped."

"What? Why?"

"If you didn't put the new lock on the door, who did? We suspect growers have been using your land. They might have helped themselves to one or more remote outbuildings." Clearly the state police hadn't gotten this far in their search or had been only focused on finding marijuana fields. Otherwise, they would have contacted Darby and asked permission to search the icehouse.

Luckily, the tree limb Darby had tripped on was only a fallen branch. It could have been worse. Much worse.

He sniffed the air but smelled no identifying meth lab stench. The air carried only the natural, earthy aromas of the forest floor mingling with the pine.

At least he'd buckled on his duty belt after making love to Darby instead of locking it in his truck. He carried his gun. Unofficially on the clock. "Just to confirm, we're still on your property?"

"Oh, yeah. I own the entire shoreline of Nippletop Lake. You have my permission to do whatever you think is necessary." She handed him her key ring.

Her consent made legally searching the building easy.

"Will you shoot off the lock if the key isn't on the ring?" she asked.

He refrained from rolling his eyes. "You watch too much television."

She scowled, but her tone remained bland. "Do you think this is Red Beard's doing?"

He studied the path, searching for anomalies. "If I'm wrong, I'm erring on the side of caution. Come on."

He backtracked to the limb Darby had kicked aside. It was the right length for what he needed. He searched the area for a non-poison ivy vine. Creeping snowberry. Perfect.

"What are you doing?"

"Making a tool to check for a tripwire."

He pulled a length of vine from the ground, then tied one end to the branch. The scent of wintergreen filled the air. He knotted the other end several times to give weight to the natural ribbon. Something in a brighter color would have worked better, but he would have to be more vigilant as he used his home-made tripwire detector. Which meant Darby needed to stay put. He wouldn't be able to focus if he worried about her.

"I need you to stay here," he said, as he tested his makeshift tool.

"Shouldn't I go back to the lodge and call the state police?"

"Let's see what I find first."

"Whoever padlocked the door on my icehouse trespassed on posted property. Why wouldn't I call the authorities?"

"Because you've got me, and I am law enforcement. Let me determine what's going on. It might be nothing."

"Okay," she replied, but she didn't appear happy.

"I'll be careful," he assured her. "The boys need their father."

He strode away from her, holding the branch ahead of him, the creeping snowberry dangling with every step. The vine didn't catch on anything. The waving leaves would have stopped if they'd encountered a tripwire.

He propped the branch against the wall while he studied the padlock. Carbon steel, if Cam guessed correctly. Impervious to bolt cutters. Whoever placed it meant business. Despite what he'd told Darby, if none of her keys worked, he might have to shoot off the lock if he wanted to access the building.

Unless the enormous doors facing the lake weren't secured.

One step—key—at a time. He methodically tried every key on the ring, even if one appeared too large for the lock. Darby did not possess the key. He retrieved his tripwire detector and made his way to the double doors once used by horses hauling sleighs heavy with ice harvested from the lake.

A padlock also secured these doors, but it was not an industrial-strength one. Again, Cam tried every key on Darby's ring. Nothing. He searched for a rock to smash the lock.

The creeping snowberry vine caught on something. He stopped. Someone had strung fishing line, barely visible against the rusty fir needles carpeting the ground, across the path. He used his branch to prod the ground on the other side of the boobytrap. Nothing happened. He stepped over the tripwire. Nothing happened. He found a rock. Several blows later, the padlock yielded. He performed a visual check on the door. Everything appeared safe.

The doors creaked open.

The open doors provided the only interior light. Ankle-deep sawdust covered the floor. Higher mounds defined the corners. The space did not smell moldy. Giant, deadly looking tongs hung on one wall, rusty oversized saw blades on another. Cam pulled his flashlight off his duty belt and aimed the light toward the rafters. Yeah. Hooks. Something probably not needed for an ice harvest. But drying marijuana? Oh yeah.

He lowered his light to the floor. One couldn't dry weed without losing a few brittle leaves. And there they were.

Time to call the state police.

Cam checked his cell phone on the off chance a signal had penetrated the wilderness. Nope.

He closed the doors and, using his tripwire detector, made his way back to Darby, who'd remained right where he left her.

"We need to call the troopers," he said. "Someone has used your icehouse as a drying shed."

Hours later, they sat on Cam's deck, eating dinner. Darby had done something right when she'd had Cam grill so many chicken breasts the previous evening. She'd also made a pasta salad. They didn't have to think about cooking. Her pre-planning had paid off, given how long they'd been with the state police, followed by Cam's long phone conversation with his captain.

They'd earned their Moonsinger and water-front dinner. The peeper choir sang in full concert mode, backed by crickets and an occasional bullfrog providing bass. Mosquitoes hummed a harmony.

Cam bit into his cold chicken. "This is really good. Will you marry me?"

Darby was almost as tired of his fake marriage proposals as she was his put-downs. His fault finding. She forced a laugh anyway. They both needed to relax. She would treat this version of a proposal as a joke. "Didn't we have this discussion?"

"No, I'm serious. If you can cook like this, you're a keeper."

"I'm serious, too," she lied. "Didn't we decide on names for our children?"

He speared a yellow pepper chunk from the pasta salad. "Remington, maybe, but no son of mine is going to be named Oswegatchie."

Now what foolishness did he have up his sleeve? The Oswegatchie River flowed through the Adirondacks, but never into their conversations. "We didn't discuss that name."

"And we won't either because the name is off the table. Now, about getting married."

He always returned to making their relationship permanent.

"All you have to do is say the word, and we'll go to Elizabethtown and get our marriage license."

She struggled to keep the tone playful. "Bureaucracy can't be that easy."

"Getting married is. My sister blabbed every detail to the whole family when she got married. All we need are photo IDs, like our driver's licenses, and our birth certificates."

"And you made sure I took mine with me when I came to stay with you." She should have known he had an ulterior motive beyond protecting her from identity theft. "You are a sneaky man, Cameron Winehouse."

"No, I told you on our first date I fell in love with you the first time I saw you."

A loon perfectly timed its laugh. Distant coyotes howled their disagreement.

"Three days ago?" Darby focused on cutting her chicken into yet smaller pieces.

"Okay, I understand. I'll wait."

"I don't think you do." She used her fork to poke a green pea from the hole of a sliced black olive. "A part of me says, 'Yes! Let's do it!'"

"But you're afraid sex is making you stupid."

He'd been listening.

"Yeah. Because the sex is great," she admitted.

But that's only part. She clenched her teeth to keep from starting an argument. She was tired. Everything bothered her.

"Making love with you is transcendental." His fork clattered to his plate. He clasped her hands and rubbed the base of her ring finger with his thumb. "I want to get you a ring."

She should have pulled free from his grasp, but she couldn't summon the energy. "Will you wear one if we get married?"

She'd already noticed he didn't wear a wristwatch.

"I plan to. Maybe I'll have your name and our wedding date tattooed on my ring finger, too."

While the ink on his body fascinated her, the idea of someone sticking needles into her skin repulsed her. If he wanted her to reciprocate the offer, he could wait until palm trees flourished in the High Peaks.

The coyotes yipped again. Darby couldn't suppress her shudder.

Cam released her hand. "They're not that close to us."

"I know. You've made me paranoid about everything."

His expression turned intense. "I don't want you being paranoid. I want you to be cautious. Illegal growers have been using your property and those guys are dangerous. The tripwire the state troopers dismantled might have looked amateurish, but those wooden stakes falling on your head could kill you."

She'd seen the multi-pronged clump of tree branches honed to deadly points and rigged to impale anyone who tripped the fishing line. The image of what the boobytrap could have done to Cam—to anyone—made her sick.

Camp Nippletop would never be hers, would never become The Write Place Retreat while the growers used the land and outbuildings as if they were the owners.

She closed her eyes and swallowed her rising nausea. "I'm going to lose everything."

"Don't think like that. We're going to get this guy." Cam swatted a mosquito on his forearm as if to prove his point. "Look at me."

She opened her eyes.

"We're going to stop him and put his ass in prison. You're going to renovate your buildings. Famous people like Stephen King and James Patterson and... Nora Roberts will flock to your place in the Adirondacks. You are going to run the best damn writing retreat in the country."

His fierce tone warmed her. He'd armed her with pepper spray and cordless phones. Tonight, he believed in her.

But earlier in the day? She'd written a list of her transgressions. According to Cam.

The nausea faded, but her appetite fled with it. Not that she'd been especially hungry. She wasn't anything except tired. So tired. The tension from the past several hours while the troopers worked the crime scene at the icehouse had seeped into her bones. She slumped in her chair.

"Talk to me."

She could barely hear Cam over nature's raucous opera. She shrugged. "I have nothing to say. It's been a long day, and I have to get up early again tomorrow for work."

"Did you talk to the attorney?"

Right. There'd been too much going on. The mundane had to wait. "I did. He said I could draw a salary and hire people to clean. He recommended Astin's former housekeeper. I'll give her a call tomorrow."

"Are you going to give your notice at the diner?"

"Do I have to decide tonight?" she snapped. At least he hadn't asked how much money she'd be taking from the trust for herself.

Cam seemed taken aback. "No. I don't mean to push you."

Yet all afternoon he'd picked at everything. *Give your notice, buy boots, you need fancy electronic locks at the camp, repost the property boundaries with your name and address. Bear spray. Cordless phones. Too much TV.* Maybe she wasn't having sex right, either.

She stood. "I'm done eating."

She carried her dirty dishes to the kitchen. Right now, she wanted her bed. The one in her apartment. Alone time. People surrounded her all day at the diner. People and noise. The solitary time she'd spent alone at the camp had been nice. *I could hear myself think,* she thought, as she scraped her uneaten food into the garbage before loading the plate into his dishwasher.

Cam followed her and slid his arms around her waist. "Stop thinking so loud."

"How can you hear what I'm thinking when I can't?" She stiffened under his touch. If he only knew. . .

His hands rested beneath her breasts. "What's bothering you?"

She thought she'd hidden her irritation. "Bothering me?"

"Babe, you're as chilly as a block of ice."

Babe? Being called a generic term of endearment made her feel nameless. Interchangeable.

"Darby," she reminded him.

"What?"

"My name is Darby, not Babe. Or Baby."

He turned her to face him. "You think I don't know who's in my arms?" He dropped a kiss on her forehead. "Or do you just not like nicknames? Oh. Wait. You called me honey."

Her only experience with being called a nickname comprised slurs regarding her weight—Dumpy Lumpy Darby. Dumbo Darby. Darby Lard-ass. Lardy.

"Darby-Baby," Cam revised the words of a Christmas song as he sang and attempted to dance with her. "Can I come in your chimney tonight?"

She groaned. "You're bad." She didn't need to try when she trod on his toes. She'd never learned to dance. Hadn't gone to her high school proms. Held the record for being the lushest, most full-blown blossoming wallflower at family wedding receptions.

"You make me a better man. Tell me what's wrong."

"I am not an airhead."

He stopped waltzing. "No, you're not. Where is that coming from?"

"Sometimes I feel as if I don't measure up to your expectations." The words should have stuck in her throat, but they came out slick as bacon grease on the grill at the diner. She hated her insecurities and the way they intruded every time she thought she could be happy.

Cam steered her into the living room. He sat in his recliner and pulled her into his lap.

"I'm too heavy—"

"Stay put." His arms were once again around her waist. "I'm going to tell you what I adore about you. The things you do right."

Her face heated.

"You kiss like a goddess. You listen when people offer advice. Maybe you don't take their advice, but you listen, and you consider it. Do you know how much I appreciated that you stayed put while I investigated the icehouse? You carry your OC spray on you and would have doused me when I frightened you in the boathouse. You're staying with me at least until we can get the illegal growers. Hopefully longer. I love the sexy sounds you make while I'm inside you."

His mouth on hers tasted of garlic from the chicken marinade and pasta salad. When he ended the kiss, he rested his forehead against hers. "You gave me a Captain Planet coffee mug."

Her irritation eased.

"But you still need boots for hiking in the forest. And to give Chuck your notice. You're exhausted. If you didn't have to be at the diner at six, you could get more sleep. You could spend your workday at the camp. Well, if the people you hire to work are with you."

"Then I do have a few redeeming qualities. Sometimes I wonder why you're with me unless you need someone to boss around." Admitting her lack of self-confidence to him increased her anxiety. But better now, three days into their relationship, than later on when they were more invested. If they lasted that long enough to have a later on.

"Oh, God." Cam tightened his hold on her. "Don't—just don't. I'm sorry if I made you feel inadequate. You're one of the most competent women I know. I mean, look at how you asked me to grill all the chicken yesterday, while you made the pasta salad. 'Meals for the rest of the week,' you said. 'Take some for your lunches.' You plan ahead. That's why you're going to be successful at running your retreat."

Great. She'd make a good wife. She tried to extract herself, but he wouldn't release her.

"I love the whole Darby Remington package. The magnificent body, beautiful smile, and wicked sense of humor. You're smart. You're the woman of my dreams." He kissed her again.

She broke off the kiss and rested her head on his shoulder. That spot on his body could have been custom made just for her.

He continued as if he hadn't paused to kiss her. "I know I sound crazy, but I swear I fell in love with you the moment I saw you. I have never felt this way before. Sometimes the intensity of how I feel scares me because I'm acting irrationally. I worry I'm coming across as a stalker or a creep. You know, the guys on the news who claim, 'if I can't have her, no one can,' and part of me, some Neanderthal corner of my lizard brain accepts their logic. Agrees with their possessiveness.

And that scares me even more because I would never do anything to harm you."

He curled a lock of her hair around his index finger. "I respect and love how you're coming into your own. I want to be your... your helpmate. The man you turn to when something frustrates or excites you. I not only want you to be there for me, I want to be there for you. Like today at the icehouse. Thank God you didn't go wandering around there by yourself." He shuddered. "When I think about what could have happened—promise me you won't go wandering around until all the buildings are cleared."

"Okay, I won't." She wasn't stupid. That boobytrap scared the snot out of her.

"Say it."

"I won't inspect any of my outbuildings that haven't been checked by law enforcement, not even the ones I visited with Chatham."

He made a heck of a speech. How could she not want to spend the rest of her life with a man who understood her so well? Who claimed to cherish her? All the actions and attitudes that bothered her—they stemmed from his concern for her. The newness of having someone in her life who prioritized her bewildered her. Oh, her parents were great, but they were Mom and Dad. Her siblings were busy with their own lives. If she needed them, truly needed them, she could count on them. Cam wanted to occupy a different space. A niche he'd carved out for himself.

"I won't mention marriage again," he said. "Okay? We'll take it one day at a time. And when you're ready, let me know. Okay?"

"And one night?" Her voice warbled. No way was she giving up sex with him.

"Every night."

CHAPTER THIRTEEN

Cam didn't make his way home until well after midnight. Darby had left the stove hood light on for him. He usually appreciated her thoughtfulness, but for a moment, he resented her intrusion into his space. He couldn't shed his clothes or knock around because he didn't want to disturb her sleep. She still had a week of working at the diner, burning her candle at both ends.

He unbuckled his duty belt. Tonight, he couldn't bear its twenty-plus-pound weight.

He grabbed a Moonsinger from the fridge and wandered out to the deck, where he stood at the rail and stared at the moon's reflection on the pond's surface. No way he could sleep. Not yet. Not after —

He sipped his beer.

Behind him, the screen door creaked. "Cam?"

Darby must have been waiting for him.

He didn't say anything. He heard her pad across the bare wooden deck floor.

"Do you want company?"

"No." The single syllable struggled to leave his throat.

She hesitated, then said: "Okay. I'll be in bed if you change your mind." She stood on her toes and kissed the corner of his mouth.

Her sleepy scent knocked something loose in his brain. A memory of the first time he'd seen her.

He abandoned his beer to follow her. He caught her arm as she opened the screen door. His mouth crashed down on hers.

He needed her. In a very elemental way. He fondled her breasts as he plundered her mouth. She didn't try to stop him or slow him down or take control. She yielded. Welcomed him.

Oh God, her soft skin undid him. So soft. Like the oversized, wash-worn t-shirt she wore. He tugged at its hem, intending to pull the garment over her head. The material parted, leaving Darby and her softness exposed to the cool night air.

He managed to lower her to the floor. Open his pants. Thrust inside of her. Lose himself in her softness. Her goodness.

She didn't resist. Didn't try to push him off. She wrapped her arms and legs around him, like the softest silk. Strong. Resilient. Nearly unbreakable. Soft.

Today, tonight, had been hard. So hard. Harder than the ancient rocks forming the Adirondacks. And she, she was the opposite of everything that had gone wrong that day. She was a balm for his pain.

Too late he realized he wasn't wearing a condom. He'd never fucked a woman without protection and found the sensations were intense. He needed intense. He needed intensity to pierce the numbness his job had required that day.

Coming inside Darby equaled praying.

He was a beast. No better than the animals that had —

"I'm sorry," he muttered.

"Never apologize for letting me comfort you."

"I hurt you." His self-inflicted guilt intensified. "I didn't use protection. I'm sorry, I—"

He tried to ease out of her, but she tightened her legs around him. "How bad?"

"Oh God." His voice broke. She knew. How did she know?

"Search and rescue?"

He nodded.

Darby waited.

Darby. His safe place. His haven. His right place. He could tell her. What he'd seen. His thoughts. What he'd felt. His rage.

"She was only six years old," he choked out. "They didn't keep their eye on her. Who lets a six-year-old kid run around unsupervised?"

The lump in his throat doubled in size. Tripled. Ballooned. Forcing everything upward. Until his eyes started leaking.

"I found her. What was left after the coyotes—"

He buried his face in Darby's neck and let go.

Cam's harsh sobs tore through Darby to her marrow. His hands clutched at her. His body shuddered atop hers. Hot tears pooled in the hollows of her collarbone, the overflow trickling across her breasts. She could only hold him close. Tight. Let him vent the agony he'd hidden within himself.

This man. This amazing man. He was a hero, although he would deny it with every cell of his being. Not only a hero for her, but for others who would never recognize what it cost him to be strong for them.

She loved him. Why did she hesitate to marry him? Tonight proved he held nothing back from her. He'd allowed her to see the real

Cameron Winehouse. The real man was far more attractive than the man who faced the world every day. Additional time would only intensify her love.

He stilled. Rolled away from her but lay on his back next to her. She probably had marks on her butt from the deck flooring.

"Sorry," he muttered again.

Darby grasped his hand. Twined her fingers with his. "Sorry because you mourned a little girl you tried to save?" Then, softly, she added: "I'm glad I was here for you."

He squeezed her fingers.

A breeze rustled in the pines, freshening the night air. Peepers serenaded the moon with their mating calls. Crickets counted out the next day's temperature. All the usual summer night sounds in the Adirondacks.

Until coyotes yipped in the distance.

Cam's hand tensed.

Darby wished she practiced magic so she could ease him.

"Thank you," he said. "For being here. Giving me space. Not freaking out when I attacked you without using a condom."

Oh yeah. *That.* She hadn't realized the difference until he'd climaxed. Until the difference flooded her. "No worries," she murmured. "I had my appointment at the clinic today. I decided on an IUD."

She'd planned a celebration, but when he didn't show up around his usual time and didn't call, she figured something had happened. This was her life now. Never sure when he'd be home. Always being afraid he might never come home.

Cam had told her only one New York State Forest Ranger had ever died in the line of duty, and that being a ranger ranked as one of the safest law enforcement jobs.

She still worried.

Then something like this happened. Something where he should have been a hero, but nature circumvented his intention. An event so disturbing, it disrupted his very soul.

Worst of all, she didn't know what to do. How to console and comfort him. All she could do was listen. Be there for him for whatever he needed. He could have hurt her when he made love to her tonight. He might argue that he hadn't made love to her but had used her for sex. He might even call the act the f-word. But she knew in her heart, knew deep in her bones that he'd been making love to her, finding solace in her body. Hers. No one else's.

She was strong enough to be at his side for the rest of her life.

"Don't try to appease me because you're sorry for me," Cam grumbled. He hadn't moved. His uniform pants remained undone and partially lowered. The peepers continued to mock the night. Darby curled her naked body against him, probably seeking warmth, because she otherwise couldn't want to be near him after what he'd just done to her.

"I don't feel sorry for you. I love you. Let's go to Elizabethtown on your next Tuesday off and get our marriage license. We can get married on Wednesday." She rested her head on his chest. "I don't need a big, fancy, overblown wedding. I don't want a wedding the way people have them these days. We can find a JP and a couple of strangers for witnesses and—"

He yanked her body up so he could kiss her. She loved him. He hadn't done anything to scare her off. Just the opposite. She should be screaming and running into the woods after what he'd done. Instead, he blessed the day the convict escaped from the prison, which led him to her. If some god or goddess somewhere wanted a sacrifice, he would make one. Unless it involved harming or relinquishing Darby. He would risk the wrath of every deity to keep her safe.

He tightened his embrace as the memory of the child—the remains of the little girl—flashed in his head. Nature had extracted enough human sacrifice that day.

Now if he could only find a graceful way to either finish removing his clothes or pulling up his pants and boxers. Mindless passion had consequences, awkwardness being the first.

"As much as I love you," Darby said, "the deck is uncomfortable. I probably have splinters in my butt. Why don't we move to a chaise or a bed?"

She rolled away from him and clambered to her feet.

He watched her amble to the kitchen door, her big, gorgeous ass pale as a winter moon beckoning the ocean tides.

She scooped up the remnants of her torn t-shirt. "Cleaning rag," she murmured. She didn't need to wear anything except him in his bed.

"Did you say you got an IUD today?" he asked, as he adjusted his pants.

"I did." She held the screen door for him. "The clinic said an IUD would protect against pregnancy for five years, but if I want to get pregnant, they could remove it and I should have no trouble."

Pregnant. Babies. Toddlers. His stomach clenched again. He wanted to be a father, especially since meeting Darby. He wanted Sally Stone's prediction of two sons to be real. But how did parents handle loss? How could they survive the agony of something happening to their offspring? He would never forget the parents' faces as he'd told them that their child, their beautiful daughter...

He staggered to the deck rail and puked into the shrubbery.

The screen door slammed. A gentle hand rubbed circles on his back. He'd lost his lunch earlier. Nothing remained in his stomach, but the emptiness didn't matter.

The cramping ceased. He straightened.

Darby linked elbows with him. "Let's get you inside. You've had a rough day."

Fifteen minutes later, he wore fresh boxers. Darby had left him alone to shower. To brush his teeth, trying to banish the sour taste. He found her waiting outside the bathroom door wearing another t-shirt, which clung to her nipples like a second skin.

She handed him his Captain Planet mug.

His empty stomach roiled. "I don't need coffee."

"No, you don't. This is chamomile tea. The hot water will settle your stomach and the chamomile will relax you."

No wonder he didn't smell coffee, but something apple-y. Where did she find tea? He sure as hell hadn't bought any.

"I like to have a cup sometimes before I go to bed." Darby read his mind.

Ah. Living together included funky teas.

Instead of heading to the bedroom, he went to the living room. He avoided his recliner to settle on one end of the sofa. Darby parked on the other end, cradling a cup in her hands. She said nothing. She merely sat, silent and still.

For him.

He sipped the tea. Not bad. Not something he would ask for, but Darby had brewed it for him and served it with his favorite superhero. Cam couldn't deny her.

Being indoors muted the night sounds, but not enough. The yips of celebrating coyotes penetrated the walls, taunting him for his failure.

His hand shook as he placed the mug on the coffee table. He needed something to distract him.

Then he remembered. He had something important to tell Darby. "I spoke to the troopers this morning."

"Did they have anything new to say?"

"They believe they've identified Red Beard and want us to look at mug shots to see if we can pick out his picture. They found a match for the fingerprints found in your apartment in their database, but want visual ID, too."

The break-in at her apartment seemed long ago. So much had happened since then. He needed to focus on their future, on the living, not on the child he couldn't save. Look forward. He couldn't have done anything differently.

Tomorrow. Darby had given him the gift of tomorrow. The gift of a future.

There would be other people he couldn't save. He knew that. The girl hadn't been the first, only the most heart-wrenching because of her age, because her parents had been careless. No, not the first and most likely not the last. Cam had seen suicides and death from the cruel elements of the High Peaks.

And the cautionary tales of the people who vanished forever. In 1971, eight-year-old Dougie Legg wandered away from Camp Santanoni, never to be seen again. Later, when Cam became a ranger, he learned the disorganized search for Dougie resulted in the DEC coordinating all future search and rescue efforts.

The Adirondacks claimed another child today anyway.

"Cam?" Darby's soft voice broke into his thoughts.

He tried to shake his head into being present with her. "I'm sorry."

"It's okay. When do the state police want us to look at the mug shots?"

"Promise me you will never let the boys outside alone." He couldn't disguise the hoarseness in his voice.

"We'll have a fenced-in play yard for them, too."

Darby's calm tone did little to soothe him.

"Say it."

"I swear I will never let the boys play outside alone. Drink your tea." She raised her bright yellow mug to her mouth and sipped.

"We can go tomorrow after work," he said, after gulping the dregs. "Or you can go right after your shift. Independent identification."

"Okay. I'm going to skip going to the camp and finish packing."

A moment's respite from his concerns. "Were you serious when you said you would marry me?"

"Yes."

"You won't change your mind between now and next Tuesday?"

"No. I've told you before. Once I set my mind to something, I see it through. So get used to the idea of having a wife. You're stuck with me."

Chapter Fourteen

Monday, June 26, 2000

Darby stood in Cam's kitchen, preparing to cook dinner. Cam estimated he might be home by four. They were both anxious about their trip to the county seat in the morning.

She'd considered calling her mom and sharing her plans but resisted the urge. She and Cam were eloping. Once she had the lodge at the camp in shape, they could throw a big party and call it a wedding reception. Maybe she could get Chuck to cater. Hah! Her parents—the parents of the bride—could help pay for that if they wanted.

Darby couldn't wait to be Mrs. Cameron Winehouse. She had as much to learn about being a good wife to him as she had about operating a writing retreat. Not that Cam didn't have a lot to learn about being a good husband to her, because he did. They could learn together.

For a change, she'd dry-rubbed boneless chicken breasts with Dinosaur Bar-B-Que Cajun Foreplay seasoning, then diced the meat into cubes. Cam could pack grilled kabobs for his lunches. He could eat the cold chicken and veggies with his fingers. She'd seen his string cheese, bags of nuts, and power bars. He packed bite-sized portable protein every day.

She found metal skewers in a kitchen drawer and began threading them with pineapple, chunks of onion, red bell pepper, mushrooms, and cubed chicken. She'd already ignited the grill. Once half a dozen kabobs rested on the platter, she used her hip to nudge open the door to the deck.

And nearly dropped the platter when she found Red Beard stretched out on a chaise.

"What are you doing here?" Her heart crammed into her throat, and her voice squeaked.

He'd found her. He must have been following her.

"We need to talk, Ms. Remington."

She sucked in oxygen to steady her pulse and her voice. "How did you get here?" She hadn't heard a vehicle pull up.

His teeth flashed dingy yellow amid his rust-colored facial hair. "Doesn't matter. What matters is I tried to do business with you, and you called the cops."

"The forest ranger comes with the territory." She carefully set the platter on the grill's shelf before it fell from her shaking hands. "The land is mine, and so is he."

"I'm not talking about the park narc. I'm talking about the troopers."

"Someone broke into my apartment and left a threat. The Saranac Lake police brought in the state police." Who were less than a mile up the road. For the first time in her life, she wished she carried a cell phone.

"You made Ranger Rick snoop around where he didn't belong."

"My property," she reminded Red Beard. "If I say he belongs, he belongs. There are six million acres in the Adirondack Park. You don't need mine for your enterprise."

He ignored her. "Then the troopers raided my drying shed."

"My icehouse." She corrected as she slipped her fingers into her pocket. She still wore the jeans she'd worn at the camp. The pair with the defense spray in the pocket. She slid the tube into her palm. "I expect my fiancé home any minute."

"I wouldn't count on it. A hiker on the Trap Dike is overdue."

Chills skittered through Darby and her stomach cramped. The Trap Dike was one of the most treacherous hikes in the park. If a hiker hadn't returned in a timely manner, the forest rangers would mount a search and rescue operation. Which meant Cam could be occupied for hours. Which meant she would be alone with an unhappy Red Beard for the foreseeable future.

She didn't want to stick around to find out what direction his unhappiness would take.

"How did a fat chick end up with a forest ranger? He must be really hard up or he really wants to get his hands on your property."

If anyone else had said that to her, she might have quipped something about their sex life. Not Red Beard.

He swung his feet to the deck. "I'm disappointed with the way you've been treating your business partner."

"And who would that be?" She struggled to remain calm.

She opened the lid on the grill. A tsunami of heat rolled out. She continued to act as if a criminal visiting her at home didn't rattle her. The kabobs needed to go on the grill. Nothing unusual. Too bad she'd threaded the skewers with chicken and veggies. They'd make a nice weapon.

Except he could turn the skewers on her.

No. She needed to get away. She had defense spray in her hand.

"I'm not staying for dinner, but thanks for the invitation," Red Beard said. "Your shish kabobs will be lumps of charcoal by the time your boyfriend gets home."

"You're right. I should wait for Cam before I put the food on." She closed the lid on the grill and retrieved the platter. "I'll stick these in the fridge. I'll be back in a minute."

She hoped he didn't catch the terror in her voice as she tried to project calm.

"I don't think so," Red Beard said.

"I don't want to leave the chicken out. Poultry is tricky." *And I don't want Cam's lunches contaminated when I dose you with pepper spray.*

She wanted her car keys. Then she could spray Red Beard and run for her car. The state police headquarters was barely a mile away. Ray Brook, according to Cam, was safer than Nippletop, where the isolation made her more vulnerable.

She miscalculated Red Beard's speed. His large palm slapped against the screen door. "I said no."

She needed to break away from him. Run, when her body resisted running. Maybe she could dose him, grab her keys, dose him again...

"What do you want from me?"

He'd trapped her between his hefty body and the door. He stunk of unwashed clothes. She wasn't tall enough to hit him over the head with the platter. And clutching it prevented her from using her pepper spray.

He leered.

Annoyance flared. Some guys thought "the fat chick" would be grateful for male attention. She wasn't that fat chick. *That* fat chick would hesitate to sacrifice the food in her hands. *This* fat chick had no choice.

She flung the contents upward. The kabobs hit Red Beard in the face. The platter shattered as it hit the deck.

Red Beard yelled, "What the fuck?" and grabbed for her.

She closed her eyes, held her breath, and hit the button on the pepper spray.

Red Beard howled.

Darby ducked under his arm and ran. She opened her eyes and shrieked as she pounded down the deck stairs.

Not to the woods. Running into the woods would be stupid. She took the easiest, most direct route to the trooper barracks. Driveway, then road. She stopped screaming, saving her breath for her getaway. A stitch attacked her side, but she didn't slow down. Luckily, she still wore her sneakers. She had no idea how long the pepper spray would incapacitate Red Beard. She ran past a rusty truck with mud-covered license plates parked at the end of Cam's driveway.

Cam's road didn't draw much traffic, so she wouldn't find help there. Her heart would burst in her chest before she made it to the trooper barracks. Once Red Beard recovered, he would come after her, and he could have a gun. She hadn't seen one, but that didn't mean anything. And she didn't know how much pepper spray remained in the tiny tube she still clutched. She should have paid more attention to the packaging.

She stopped to catch her breath. The spray gave her a few minutes lead time. She didn't want to waste a second, but unless she could breathe, it wouldn't matter whether Red Beard shot her, or she keeled over into the ditch and drowned. She bent over, her hands on her upper thighs, gulping in air as best she could. She was not made for marathons. Not even to save her own life.

Had she remembered to tell Cam she loved him before she'd left for work at the diner that morning? That she looked forward to tomorrow and getting their marriage license? She wanted to be married to him. Have those two boys Sally Stone had predicted. If he wanted to name the second son Oswegatchie, fine.

What if she died without him knowing? Believing she'd been careless?

She didn't want to die. Not until she'd had a chance to live.

She straightened. She had no idea how much time had passed since she sprayed Red Beard, but she needed to stop wasting her getaway window. She resumed jogging toward the highway.

Thank God I'm not needed for the Trap Dike rescue, Cam mused as he drove home. He'd already dealt with a group of hikers who thought their dogs should be able to run wild, something not allowed in certain areas of the High Peaks. They had insisted Cam had infringed on their constitutional rights when he reminded them of the leashed-dog regulation. Their discussion had become so heated, Cam issued citations for everyone in the group except the dogs, because the dogs weren't to blame for their owners. When one hiker ripped up his ticket and threw the scraps to the ground, Cam calmly wrote him a second one for littering.

If Cam had to choose one task over the other, he would have chosen the rescue. People being rescued were grateful, not argumentative. The location of the stranded hiker meant the state police aviation unit with its helicopters had been called in. The extraction didn't require all-hands-on-deck. Cam could go home to Darby, his soon-to-be wife.

He turned off Route 86. A figure jogging in the distance re-sembled Darby. Since meeting her, it seemed he saw the woman he loved everywhere.

Except this woman dashed into the middle of the road and waved her arms.

Shit. The runner *was* Darby.

Cam sped up until he pulled even with her, then slammed on the brakes and shoved the transmission in park. He hopped out of the truck as soon as he unlatched his seatbelt.

"What's wrong?" Shattered fragments of worst-case scenarios flashed through his mind.

Darby's chest heaved, as if she'd been running for miles. "Red Beard," she managed.

"Where?" Cold dread surged into every crevice of his body. "The house? My house?"

Darby nodded.

"*Fuck.*"

"Sprayed him," she gasped.

Everything in him wanted to head to his house and confront the man who'd terrorized Darby. Instead, his training kicked in.

"Come on." He led Darby to the truck and helped her climb inside. He used his radio to call the state police and explain the situation. "I'll need backup."

"Stay put," the dispatcher instructed Cam. "Let us handle this."

The fuck he would. This bastard had come after his woman in his house. Cam still wore his duty belt—complete with handcuffs, OC spray, and, most importantly, his Sig Sauer.

"Ranger Winehouse, let us handle this," the dispatcher repeat-ed. "Illegal growers and home invasions are our jurisdiction."

He clenched his teeth. The dispatcher was right, but damn it, the bastard had come after Darby in the one place Cam had thought she'd be safe.

"Stay on with me, Ranger Winehouse," the dispatcher said.

"I need to wash my hand," Darby said at the same time. "I got pepper spray on it."

Cam glanced at her. Her pale face and shaking voice concerned him. "Keep your fingers away from your eyes. Don't use the bathroom until you've washed your hands."

He tried to get her to relax, to accept that he would protect her with his life. "Remind me to tell you about the guy who subdued a prisoner with OC spray, then forgot to wash his hands before peeing. His wife was really unhappy."

"I heard she was really relieved," the female dispatcher contradicted in a dry tone.

Yesterday, Darby would have laughed. At least she wasn't crying. Her breathing slowed toward normal. Her trembling eased.

He unsnapped his holster for easier access to his sidearm.

"How long ago did you spray the suspect?" the dispatcher asked.

"I don't remember."

"Can you give the state police an estimate?" Cam struggled to use as gentle a voice as he could. Darby didn't deserve his rage.

"No. I sprayed him and ran. I thought about going for my car keys. Getting away seemed smarter."

"You did everything right," Cam assured her.

"His truck. He parked on the road, so I didn't hear him pull up."

Bile filled Cam's throat. As much as he wanted to hear the sequence of events, he waited. The troopers needed to question Darby. She would have to keep reliving her terror with them. He reached across the console and took her hand. Her left hand.

"I kept the pepper spray on me, just like I promised. What should I do with the can?" She held up her right hand and uncurled her fingers. The OC spray rested in her palm.

A state police cruiser raced past them, lights flashing, distracting him from answering right away. The troopers weren't using sirens.

"Hold on to it."

"Ranger Winehouse," the dispatcher interrupted. "Please bring Ms. Remington to the barracks. She'll need to make a statement."

As much as Cam wanted to be in on the action back at his house, the troopers wouldn't appreciate his interference. Besides, Darby needed him. He'd fucked up. He'd thought she'd be safer at his house than at her camp. His arrogance had put her at risk.

"I need to shut off the grill. And clean up the food, or else the bears will bother us," Darby said. "I'm sorry, Cam. I made a big mess on the deck. We should go back so I can clean before it becomes a problem."

"You need to report to the state police barracks, Ms. Remington," the dispatcher repeated. "I'll instruct the officers to deal with the grill."

Cam started a three-point turn when he spied a truck speeding toward him. The troopers were right behind, the siren now howling in syncopation with the flashing lights.

He had his chance. The state police might be pissed, but Cam refused to surrender his need to protect Darby. He lowered his window and pulled his gun. Aimed.

Darby's frazzled nerves frayed a bit more, as Red Beard's truck hurtled toward them. All the things she wanted to tell Cam crowded her mind. All the things she'd thought while running. Except she'd run out of time for anything more than, "I love you," before the truck barreling their way would hit and kill them.

Cam fired.

Darby swallowed a scream.

Red Beard's truck careened into the ditch.

The radio squawked as the dispatcher demanded to know what had happened.

Cam didn't respond. He aimed again.

Darby kept her mouth shut. Held her breath as the trooper approached Red Beard's truck, shouting words she couldn't process because static filled her brain. White dots flickered in her vision like visual static. She hoped she didn't do something stupid like faint.

The trooper held his gun at the ready.

Red Beard stumbled out of his truck, hands in the air.

The trooper grabbed him and shoved him against the cruiser.

Cam coolly observed the action. Darby focused on Cam. A muscle in his cheek twitched.

Dispatch kept demanding a response from Cam, who ignored the squawking.

Eventually Cam returned his gun to its holster, then radioed dispatch they were coming in.

"What's going on?" the dispatcher asked.

"I shot out a front tire," Cam admitted. "I assisted in the capture."

He finished turning his truck and drove toward Route 86.

"Are you in trouble?" Darby whispered her question.

"Maybe." Cam sounded grim. "Not as much trouble as Red Beard is in."

Darby finally stopped shaking. She still gripped the pepper spray, uncertain what to do with it. She supposed she could return the tube to her pocket once they arrived at the barracks. Unless the troopers wanted it for evidence, but she couldn't imagine why they would.

She had only a few more minutes alone with Cam before bureaucracy swallowed her. She needed to tell him. Everything. "I love you, and I worried I didn't remember to tell you how much I love you before I left for work this morning. I can't wait to be your wife. For you to be my husband. I couldn't remember if I ever actually said the words to you. And you need to know how I feel. And I was so afraid Red Beard would kill me, and you would never know I fell in love with you when you came to warn me about the escaped prisoner. You need to know. Oswegatchie is a fine name for our second son. If you want."

One corner of Cam's mouth quirked up. "I don't want. That's what I said. No Oswegatchies."

"We could call him Ozzie. We'll have Remy and Ozzie, and I can't wait to meet them."

"In a few years." He pulled into the state police parking lot. "I want as much alone time with you as I can get."

Tears leaked from her eyes. She started to rub them, then remembered the pepper spray on her hands.

Cam shut off his truck and turned to her. "Hey," he said when he realized she was crying. He used his thumbs to wipe away her tears.

"Delayed reaction," she muttered.

"You're allowed. You don't always have to be strong."

"You rescued me."

He smiled. "It's what I do. Search and rescue. Protect and preserve the natural resources of New York. You're the most important natural resource I have."

Then he kissed her, and everything in her world was right.

EPILOGUE

FRIDAY, JUNE 27, 2003 (THREE YEARS LATER)

Darby Remington Winehouse clutched the guest register to her breasts as she stood on the Write Place Retreat's wide veranda. The scent of wild iris polluted the early summer air. Bees buzzed, loons yodeled, and a critter rustled the brush at the edge of the lane. Even after three years, she still had problems believing she'd not only inherited the former great camp, but that she'd turned her vision into reality.

Sure, the past two years had seen guests in the three cabins, starting with a rowdy group of romance authors who'd wanted the "sexy orange cottage," but today was the true opening of The Write Place Retreat. No vacancies. The four suites she'd planned on the second floor of the main lodge were ready for occupancy. They'd been booked for six months. Until last week, Darby had worried she'd been too optimistic. The anxiety still made her want to vomit.

The crunch of tires on the gravel drive had her straightening her spine. She clutched the book tighter and winced at the soreness in her breasts. Stupid PMS. It was three in the afternoon. Guests could arrive at any minute. Her mood deflated as she recognized the car. Sue Stone, her former co-worker at the diner, was dropping off her daughter Sally, whom Darby had hired as a part-time maid.

Cam's DEC truck pulled in behind Sue. Why was he home so early on a Friday in June? Was there a problem? She hadn't expected him for hours.

Sue climbed out of her car, brandishing a foil-topped bottle. Sally followed. Cam exited his truck, his mirrored sunglasses reflecting Darby and the lodge.

Darby met him half-way and yanked off the offending glasses. "You're home early."

"I didn't want to miss your big day." He planted a kiss on her mouth.

"I brought bubbly to celebrate," Sue said, holding her bottle aloft. "You've worked so hard to make this happen. I confess, when you quit the diner, I had my doubts."

"Let's go inside," Darby suggested. She didn't want her incoming guests to think the lodge was party central. The retreat advertised quiet and solitude.

Once in the lobby, she returned the guest register to its proper place on the welcome counter, then polished the chrome call bell with her shirt sleeve.

She shouldn't be this nervous. Plenty of authors had come through her doors over the past two years. The four new suites were only an expansion of the facilities.

A wave of dizziness caught her by surprise. She clutched the edge of the counter for support.

"Relax," Cam said. "You've got this."

"I've got this," she repeated.

"Where do you hide your glasses?" Sue asked. "Let's pop this cork and salute a job well done before the guests arrive."

"Darby can't drink a toast with the champagne," Sally said. "It might harm the baby."

"What?" Darby and Cam spoke at the same time.

Sue muttered something that sounded like, "Here we go again."

Sally gestured toward Darby's midsection. "You're going to have a baby boy, just like I told you that morning at the diner."

"You're pregnant?" Cam's mouth fell open for a moment before he appeared to gather his wits. "Why didn't you tell me?"

"I'm not! I don't think." She took a quick inventory of how she was feeling. "Maybe?"

"Don't drink alcohol until you find out for sure," Cam rounded the counter so he could wrap his arms around her, resting both of his palms on her belly.

"Of course not," she agreed. Wow. A baby. She should have seen that one coming.

"Say it." Cam always needed her to be specific.

Darby swallowed hard. "I won't drink Sue's champagne or any other alcoholic beverage until a pregnancy test comes back negative." She could think of a lot of other things she'd be giving up, too, if Sally was right.

A vehicle pulling up to the veranda halted further discussion.

Sally peeked out the front window. She gasped. "It looks like that famous movie director." She whispered a well-known name not on Darby's list.

"You and your imagination." Sue shook her head.

The man came into the lobby carrying a large valise and a computer bag.

"Hi," Darby said as perkily as she could manage, given the way her stomach roiled.

"You should have a reservation for Lucas Stevens." The credit card he offered, however, bore the name Sally had murmured. He smiled as if he and Darby shared a secret.

As much as Darby wanted to go fan-girl on the man, she maintained what she hoped was a professional demeanor.

Half an hour later, "Mr. Stevens" was settling into his suite, Sue had left, and Sally was transferring a load of sheets from the washer to the dryer. Cam and Darby had a moment to themselves in the kitchen. He had started a pot of coffee, Captain Planet mug in hand.

"We're only five hours or so from New York City," Cam said. "Don't be surprised if you start seeing more people you may have heard of."

"He can afford to go anywhere." Darby swallowed hard. The smell of brewing coffee was getting to her. She didn't want to talk about the mystery guest. She might be pregnant, and that was more important. "About the baby—"

Cam spoke over her. "He chose to come here. You've made your dream come true."

"James Coolidge Astin's dream," she muttered.

"If you hadn't made it your own dream, none of this would have happened."

"If I built it, they would come?" She couldn't keep the snark out of her voice.

Cam laughed. "You did, and they're on their way."

I hope you enjoyed reading The Right Place.

For a free, bonus epilogue, sign up for my newsletter at https://mailchi.mp/2fb731c01319/the-right-place-bonus-epilogue

I send newsletters only twice a month, unless I have something major to share.

The Right Place is an origin story for a new series taking place at The Write Place Retreat. The first book in the series, SNOWED IN: HEAT RISES will be be available for pre-order soon.

Chef Justine Macko has lost everything and is forced to take a job in a remote region of New York's Adirondack Mountains while she reclaims herself. But a snowstorm sidelines her until she's rescued by Meade Godwin, a romance author who is wildly successful under a secret pen name, but who is ready to move on to writing "real" books while trying to find his true self.

This story is for you if you like: forced proximity, stranded, secret identities, scars, domestic staff, fish out of water, professions, and workplace romances.

Afterword

This story takes place at the turn of the 21st century. Technology wasn't what it is now. Marijuana was still illegal in New York (and as of this writing, remains illegal to grow on state land).

This book (and series) is set in the High Peaks Region of New York's Adirondack Mountains. The Adirondack Park encompasses 6 million acres, about half of which are designated forever wild. The park is bigger than Yellowstone, Everglades, Glacier, and Grand Canyon National Park combined.

Nippletop Mountain is a real place, as are Lake Placid (site of two Winter Olympics), St. Huberts, Gothics Mountain, Ray Brook, and Saranac Lake.

Nippletop Lake and Camp Nippletop are fictitious.

Adirondack Great Camps are a real thing, There are many informative websites about their history and their current role in the Adirondacks.

The story of the disappearance of eight-year-old Douglas Legg from a Great Camp is true. https://www.adirondackhub.com/story/2016/10/santanoni-unsolved-adirondack-mystery

Acknowledgements

So many people helped in the process of writing this book, I hope I can remember them all!

Random Individuals

- Amanda Baker, for info on service weapons.

- Chip Compton, Apple Valley Builders for insights on rehab.

- Scott Morales, Cops & Writers Facebook Group.

- Kristine Kipers, attorney who answered questions about the law.

New York State Department of Environmental Conservation

- Jeff Wernick, Press Office, for putting me in touch with the person whose brain I needed to pick.

- Captain Kevin Burns, Forest Ranger, Region 5 North who spent a lot of time answering a lot of questions and giving me insight on what it's like to be a forest ranger in the High Peaks of the Adirondack Mountains. His input was invaluable.

<u>Groups</u>

- The BFA Patreon Office: Angel, Rona, Kate, Anna, Lucy, Elodie, Mary, Liz L, Liz S, Christine, Azalea—if I've forgotten anyone, I'm sorry.

- The Purples: Carol, Chris F, Chris W, Gayle—besties, critique partners, goddesses.

- The Ghostwriters: Andrea, Holly, Janine, Julie, Kris, Nina—thanks for the love and laughter!

ALSO BY MJ COMPTON

<u>CONTEMPORARY SPORTS (BASEBALL) ROMANCE</u>

COLUMBIA GEMS BASEBALL ROMANCES

MISSING THE SIGNS – A second chance with the sexy baseball player who ghosted me seven years ago? Let me count the "no ways".

HIT BY HIS PITCH – I was abandoned. Stranded. Broke. Until the playboy pitcher came in for the save.

CATCHER INTERFERENCE: TAG & SKYE PART 1 – One injured catcher. One sizzling caterer. A torrid post-season game neither can afford to lose.

NO DOUBLES DEFENSE: TAG & SKYE PART 2 – What's an injured catcher to do when spring training starts without him? Losing himself in the decadence of Mardi Gras seems like a good start.

BATTING CLEANUP: TAG & SKYE PART 3 – Baseball may be the only place in life where a sacrifice is really appreciated, but catcher Tag Gentry never expected Skye Schuyler to risk everything for him.

SHIFTER- BASEBALL MASHUP NOVELLA

Shifting Home – The only shift baseball star Spike Peters knows is when players realign their defensive positions on the field. But when the most attractive woman he's ever encountered starts babbling about shifting, full moons, fated mates, and—worst of all—forever, the fastest runner in the game's first instinct is to run—straight to her bed.

SHIFTER ROMANCE

Toke Lobo & the Pack Series

MOONLIGHT SERENADE-Werewolves working for the government? Reporter Delilah Tenney must choose:the story of a lifetime or a lifetime of love.

"Compton's debut is a gripping, sexy as hell, page turner of a werewolf novel not for the faint hearted!" ~ NY Times Bestselling Author Maggie Shayne.

AND JERICHO BURNED- Lucy Callahan will do anything to save her sister, even if that means marrying a stranger. Even if that stranger is an undercover government agent out to destroy the cult holding her sister hostage. Even if that stranger is a . . . werewolf.

A Night Owl Reviews Reviewer Top Choice.

OMEGA MOON RISING- One desperate woman intent on escape. One brash werewolf determined to deny his DNA. Until his destiny becomes her deliverance.

A Night Owl Reviews Reviewer Top Choice.

Service for Sanctuary Series

BETRAYED BY THE MOON – Service for sanctuary–that was the werewolves' deal for over 200 years. Now the government is changing the rules, leaving Ethan Calhoun fighting for the only way of life he's ever known— and Selena Wolfe fighting for her life.

BEWARE OF THE MOON – One-night stands don't turn into forever unless you happen to pick-up a werewolf. She thought the hook-up was just another one-and-done. He knew she was his one-and-only. But when his mission unlocks the treacheries of her past, they are forced to put aside their differences as they battle for their lives.

BESIEGED BY THE MOON – Fated soul mates. She's a werewolf assassin in heat on a mission. He's a werewolf EMT and the father of her future children. What could possibly go wrong?

About the Author

MJ Compton grew up near Cardiff, New York, a place best known for its giant—a hoax so successful, P.T. Barnum duplicated it. The tale of the "petrified man" convinced MJ that inventing stories could be a career.

Although her 30 years working in local television included such highlights as being bitten by a lion, preempting a US President for a college basketball game, giving a three-time world champion boxer a few black eyes, and meeting her husband, MJ never lost her dream of creating her own stories.

MJ still lives in upstate New York with her husband. Music and cooking are two of her passions, and she enjoys baseball, college basketball, and sitting on her patio on summer nights to count lightning bugs, but she's primarily focused on writing.

www.ingramcontent.com/pod-product-compliance
Lightning Source LLC
Chambersburg PA
CBHW061540310726
48972CB00008B/2549